Praise for other books by Jo Ann Kiser:

THE GUITAR PLAYER AND OTHER SONGS OF EXILE

Every word here has earned its place on the page. Descriptions of Kentucky nature and contrasting city structures effortlessly draw readers into the scene, and both characters and setting pulse with life. Kiser's people are full of incisive questions about identity, family, and generational trauma, especially in relation to southern culture.

Book Life, in *Publisher's Weekly*

Each story is a microcosm of discovery and change that resonates and blossoms into unexpected revelations. They are interconnected not by characters and circumstances, but by the manner in which life evolves and transforms the perspectives and choices of each character.

D. Donovan, Senior Reviewer, *Midwest Book Review*

These stories are beautifully written with a jewel-like quality. They feature Kentucky hills as actual backdrops or as stuff of memories for some dislocated former residents coping in urban settings like Columbus, Chicago, and New York City, while recalling with fondness people and places left behind.

Vick Mickunas, Book Nook, *Dayton Daily News*

A YOUNG WOMAN FROM THE PROVINCES

This richly detailed bildungsroman, the follow up to Kiser's story collection *The Guitar Player and Other Songs of Exile*, surveys a surprising life, answering over its length the question of how its narrator, Geneva Clay of Kentucky coal country, grew from front-porch nights listening to "tree frogs and the lonely palpitating whip-poor-will" to become the kind of book-minded, art-struck New York City dreamer who describes "a celebrated Goya Christ" as a "mass of dark but luminous energy." The novel bustles with incident and vibrant, everyday life as it considers, year-by-year, Geneva's youth, from the 1940s into the bumptious 1960s, capturing long-gone people and ways of being (making "lye soap with bacon grease, lye, and water"; paging through a "Monkey Ward wishbook" agape at the "strange contraptions" of the women's underclothes).

Book Life, in *Publisher's Weekly*

Jo Ann Kiser's new novel, *A Young Woman from the Provinces*, unspools a journey to the self, the only reliable home that is everyone's birthright. At one point, young narrator-protagonist Geneva Clay looks from her pickup bed perch through the tarp framing a lost green homestead. Her view from the bed of the truck remains galvanizing, a rich, expansive past, if not locally sustainable, must be recovered and carried forward, elsewhere. ... Going home, and whether you can, is an ageless topic. In *A Young Woman from the Provinces*, Geneva Clay's movement into adulthood conjures past and present homes, sharing an irresistible tale of formal and informal education, of intellectual and personal growth.

Jane Blakelock, *Yellow Springs News*

Jo Ann Kiser is an impeccable prose stylist and a gifted storyteller. She describes natural worlds steeped in wonder: "two small cornfields shimmering green and silver in the sunlight; its steep pasturage, anchored by an ancient hickory..." This novel took Jo Ann Kiser half a century to complete. And it was well worth the wait.

Vick Mickunas, Book Nook, *Dayton Daily News*

A Young Woman from the Provinces will appeal to readers of contemporary women's fiction who especially enjoy stories of maturity and friendships. It follows the experience of Geneva, who moves from her home in backwoods Kentucky to the allure of New York City— there to hone a career, friendships, and possible romance that lead her ever deeper into growth and change. Jo Ann Kiser's poetic voice adds depth and metaphor to the atmosphere...

D. Donovan, Senior Reviewer, *Midwest Book Review*

Sunday People

a novel

Jo Ann Kiser

atmosphere press

In memoriam for Lila Weinberg and Penelope Roesing Fanning

Whose bright lives illuminated wherever and whatever they did.

THE CASKILL COMPLEX

ORSON CASKILL—store owner and philosopher; husband of
SARAH BETH; father of JEFF, CHARLENE, and Theresa;
grandfather of MELISSA; friend of FERGUS; former
lover of DARCY

Bernice—Jeff's wife
Bob—Charlene's husband
Bryan—Orson's brother
Charlene—Orson and Sarah Beth's daughter; caught between
worlds
Darcy—Orson's old flame and Melissa's dissertation adviser
Darryl—Orson's brother
Drusilla—Orson's sister, loved by Fergus
Fergus—Orson's friend; outlaw and outcast
Floyd—Theresa's husband
Jeff—Orson's son; storekeeper and guitar player
Melissa—Orson and Sarah Beth's granddaughter; Jeff and
Bernice's daughter
Pete—Orson's brother
Randall—Charlene's love interest
Susan—Orson's sister
Theresa—Orson and Sarah Beth's daughter; like her mother,
keeper of the flame
Winona—Charlene's friend

THE ALSECK COMPLEX

SARAH BETH ALSECK CASKILL—wife of ORSON; keeper
    of the flame; mother of JEFF, CHARLENE, and Theresa;
    grandmother of MELISSA

Brothers Lyman and Johnson—preachers in church estab-
    lished by Sarah Beth's ancestors
Burt—Sarah Beth's brother-in-law
Elswick—Sarah Beth's brother
Jervis—a preacher in Sarah Beth's church and an Alseck
    cousin
Jolene—Sarah Beth's sister; married to Burt
Roger—Sarah Beth's cousin

Contents

1. 1992: SUNDAY PEOPLE

ORSON

Woodrow Wilson died the year I was born. My pappy was a good Democrat, so my middle name is Woodrow. Orson Woodrow Caskill. Not many people know that. I foolishly told Fergus when we were boys and sometimes he calls me President and when he does I know he's been up to something he knows I wouldn't like so he goes whole hog and lets me know that I got no power over him. My folks, having given me the name, never mentioned it again. It's there on the birth certificate but if any of my brothers or my sister even remember that fact, they kindly let it lie. I want it put on my tombstone, though. The coming in and the going out.

I am dying. I sit here on the platform chanting and saying *amen*, but I don't think you can bargain with God, if he exists. Instead, I'm striking a bargain with my life. Yes, I have joined the church in my sixty-eighth year, letting my wife try to bargain.

Today, Sarah Beth's nephew Emile is marrying Darcy's niece Bertha. They look glossy, those two, dressed up like Little Lord Fauntleroy and Rapunzel, both now living in Pittsburgh.

Most of the Caskills and Alsecks and Wrights and Titwells seem to be here. This church is too small for all of us—some of the younger ones outdoors visiting with each other, waiting to throw rice. Good to look into the crowd sitting out front and see my son and his Bernice and their daughter and then Charlene with her two boys. Sweet thing to think of Tessie and Floyd at the house waiting for us. I thought Sarah Beth would be bothered about it when Tessie left the Baptists and joined Floyd's Methodists, but she wasn't. Across the platform on the women's side sits my wife of forty-some years, quietly listening. She don't go in for the shouting that some of the members seem to think will get them into heaven. Since I haven't been to meeting for years, I've been mightily surprised by some of my neighbors carrying on like Hottentots. I don't think they used to do that much of it or that loud. Lord have mercy, as Sarah Beth says when she throws up her hands and gives up on something. Charlene rolls her eyes and says, "Spare me." Jeff laughs and shakes his head. And Tessie goes about trying to set it right. Me, I crack another joke. Like when the finance company repossessed our furniture that summer after Char was born. I said to Fergus when he walked in the front door, "Sit down on your finger and rare back on your thumb." I remember because then I thought there was something indecent sounding about that, though I hadn't intended it that way. It's true Sarah Beth turned her head and left the room, but that was because she feels about Fergus the way she does. Fergus and I were going fishing, which was a good idea because there was no meat in the house.

The truth about us. God's truth? I tell the truth more often than not about things, but I don't always set them right. Telling the truth goes way back, maybe to the time when I lied about planting the beans in the upper cornfield. I was in a hurry to go play and just scattered them everywhere instead of poking them one by one into the dirt. Pappy didn't find out until some of them sprouted, some of the ones the birds left.

4

Instead of whipping me, as I expected, and Pappy was a good whipper, he told me that the devil would get me if I kept on lying. I must have been seven or eight. I was afraid to go to sleep every night for I don't know how long, for fear the red monster would get me. Somehow, I figured if I could see, I'd know what to do, so the problem was only at night. Didn't seem to affect my daytime behavior any. For the first time, though, I felt that real bad things could happen to you, bad things your pappy and momma couldn't stop. Including bad things that you yourself could do. There's been Fergus and the badness he gets up to, and how do I live with that? And back in the forties I went to war and I was for sure breaking commandments. Somewhere in there, though, I started keeping an account. It's not that I've never lied or been mean to someone or in some way cheated, but I always make sure I tell myself about it. If God didn't do the work, I guess I figured I would.

I am dying. I look at my family, as I'm doing right now in church, and I want them to know the truth about me, whatever that means. So here in church, where I've had no intention of listening to the preachers whoop and holler, I think I'll work at thinking how I'll tell my son who I am. And after I tell Jeff, then I'll tell Sarah Beth that I've told him so she'll know my first thought is for the family that we made together, the most important part of the truth. If an angel asked Sarah Beth to sacrifice Charlene or Jeff or Tessie—or me—she'd turn her back on that awful light.

I was at home when Charlene was born, right outside the room hearing my young wife yell like a panther. Char was the only one of our children that old Rachel the midwife delivered. I made sure there was a doctor in the picture for Jeff and then Tessie.

I had rather be out by the pond than here in this church. My own pond on that piece of property Sam Alseck gave me after I let him run up a bill for a year and a half's worth of groceries when he was out of work. Just a little patch of land at the foot of Sarvis Mountain, not big enough to be put to much use. There is an old cabin beside the pond, with wild roses growing where the yard used to be. Some of my people used to live there before Hobart Alseck, Sarah Beth's grandfather, took it over. I like to think of the pond being fed by underground water from Sarvis Creek. I sit under one of the two tall tulip poplars, the hill at my back. Some bluegills and bass in the pond—I swear I don't know how they could of got there—but I never go fishing in God's pond, as I named it, whether or not he exists. ("Maybe he's a she," my granddaughter Melissa said one Sunday, and to one of the visiting preachers, too.) It's not like my brother's pond, where the cows go to drink. His pond is kind of God's garden, surrounded by nut trees—hickory, black walnut, and, real close by, hazelnut bushes—and not too far away the huckleberry vines that bear every year, and wild honeysuckle, too, which is good for the bees. If you take the old road up the hill above my brother's pond, you come to the cove where his family plants corn and hoes it and shucks it as we did there when we were boys.

But if God's of a mind to enjoy his creation fresh from his labors, he exists at my pond. On Sunday mornings I may come to church, but Sunday afternoons after dinner I go to the pond. Whenever I tell Jeff whatever I'm going to tell him, I'll take him to the pond. He's never sat there, at least not with me. Neither has Sarah Beth or the girls. God probably eavesdrops on me because I've got in the habit of talking to myself out there. Probably gets an earful.

I'll go after Sunday dinner. Maybe my stomach will let me eat one of Sarah Beth's good meals today. I know she's making chicken and dumplings—dumplings light as spring clouds—and there will be green beans and tomatoes from the garden and cornbread with butter churned fresh yesterday evening, and something for dessert, maybe a peach cobbler since she bought some peaches from Bernice's teacher friend's son who brought them up from Georgia. I'll pay for it afterward, but it's worth it.

Jeff and Bernice, and Melissa. Tessie and Floyd, who have left their young'uns behind with Floyd's cousin. Charlene and her sons, Richard and Hazlett. Richard and Hazlett will be whispering to their mother about how they want to get back to Lexington but they will nourish their bellies plenty. I like to see them eat, and Hazlett has got back to liking me and his grandma. I don't know if Richard ever will. He's his daddy's son. That prissy snob.

I hate to see Char taking that medicine. Regular as clockwork. Sarah Beth says she might have to stay on it the rest of her life. What happened to my girl to give her that kind of mind trouble? I got up the nerve to ask her once if I was to blame, because I knew it wasn't Sarah Beth's fault. But me, I've got my ways. Like keeping Fergus as a buddy when I know they all hate him. And passing things off with a joke. Char hugged me, something I never encouraged with my girls, but she's taken to doing so lately, and said what she had probably was hereditary, remember Aunt Drusilla and Great-Granddaddy Len. My pappy told me that his ma told him that Len would all of a sudden go into a trance and then pick up where he left off several minutes later, after everybody else had moved on. It got to be a family joke. When somebody wasn't paying attention, somebody else could be counted on to say, "I believe you must be related to Granddaddy Len." Poor Drusilla, my sister, threw herself off the railway trestle at Finley Pass, down, down, down onto those steep, sharp rocks. She was dead before they got down to her. Her neck was broken, for one thing. Blood on the moss.

Theresa takes after Drusilla, only Tessie's happier, because of Floyd, I guess, who's a good man. Drusilla, who was six years older than me, nursed the birds with broken wings and the three-legged old hunting dog Pappy kept around—and Fergus. Drusilla was the only person besides me to understand that Fergus had a broken wing. She was always sweet to him and he loved her. Never cut up rough around Drusilla and

7

finally came courting her but she drew back. Thank God. After I got back from the war, Momma got talking and she told me that Drusilla had disappeared the summer of her fifth year, the year before I was born, and that when they found her seven days later curled up damp and dirty, her clothes torn, by Juniper Creek, she wouldn't talk for almost a month and she was never the same after that. It was clear to me then that I had not been able to see that Drusilla herself had a broken wing. I still wonder what happened to that five-year-old child. Maybe something darker than I in my happier moments would like to think could happen here. The day she died, my momma said to my pappy, "Well, she's at rest now, poor girl," and Pappy shook his head.

Well, it was a rough life. Pappy made a little money cutting timber—lord, how I hate it now, those big old trees are gone, gone—but mostly we lived on what we raised and what we found in the woods. At Christmastime we usually had a little sugar in the house for baking, and some of the time we had flour for biscuits, but mostly we ate cornbread from corn we took to our cousin who ran the mill over on Ransome Creek. It was a big old thing, and us boys would swim in the mill pond. I went over that way last year. Part of it's still standing, but its pond is low and full of scum. One year Momma and Drue and Pete and Bryan came down with bad cases of influenza, and Momma almost died. We couldn't afford a doctor, not even that time Pappy broke his arm. Old Rachel, the midwife, set it for him. Some winters we started running out of food. Along about March, pickings got awful slim.

Finally, when I was half growed, Pappy sold off some land and started the store. Wasn't another one around for miles that kept the goods he did. All us boys were working in the mines by then. Susan was married, and Drue was dead. When I was elected to help in the store, I was mightily relieved. Always had a dread of the mines. Ever since I was a little boy and they had a methane explosion at the Finley. Twelve men were killed, and two of them were my older cousins who had come visiting most Sundays.

***

Living above the cove, on our big flat on the south side of Sarvis Mountain. Six of us young'uns, four boys and Susan and Drue. Three left now, and my turn has come. (And then there were two little Indians and then there were none, as it says in that Agatha Christie mystery of Char's.) My family's not like Sarah Beth's, which has been around since forever. My daddy's daddy came over from Ireland after the Civil War, along with his brother, who settled somewhere in Pennsylvania (he came to visit once when I was little, riding on a big black horse and making my grandpappy cry with joy; that's all I remember), and Grandpappy came on to Kentucky, down the Ohio River. I read his diary sometimes. One of Sarah Beth's prize possessions. Well, mine, too. But Sarah Beth's the one who made a special cotton bag for it and who makes sure anybody who's privileged to look at it puts it back in the bag and returns it to the top of one of those bookshelves I made for her. Yeah, Grandpappy came on West looking for land in the Bluegrass, but it cost too much by then, so he struck out for the hills. He wrote they weren't like the hills of Ireland but more like Scotland. I'd like to go to Scotland and see for myself.

My mother's family, nobody knows. It's only as old as the memory of its oldest living people. The oldest tombstone in the Wright graveyard goes back to 1888. Pappy met her at a pie social and he bought her apple pie. He always teased her about being barefoot at the time. Her sister smoked a corncob pipe. Do my children remember?

We had a hard life, but we were a pretty satisfied bunch, I guess. Except for Drue. Sarah Beth always says to me, "I married you for that smile." But when she's mad at me, "You never tell me anything." All the older Caskills are like that. We talk with our eyes all the things that our religion told us not to say. After you do that for a while, you get out of the habit of talking about things that matter. Well, that's not entirely true. We talk about our work and our kin and our friends and politics and even, once in a while, religion. I think it was the war that got me down on religion. Although Fergus probably contributed.

***

I was walking home from school that day. The schoolhouse was down on bottomland, not by Sarvis Creek where that big old school is now but over near the big bend on Tumbling Branch. We had Naylor Hallem for a teacher—he'd finished high school over at Short Fork. He was a mean son of a gun. Threw a book at me once because I misspelled a word. Or was it because Andy Jones and me untied his horse every chance we got? But we did that after he made Drusilla cry. It must've been hard, I grant him that, teaching primer through eighth grade.

Anyway, I was on my way home, probably pretending to shoot squirrels, when I heard a hollering. I followed it off the track apiece, and there was Fergus in ragged clothes, dirty as sin, pivoting on a rope that dangled from a big stout limb. I'd seen him at school, but never said more than two words to him. He was a loner. He had been up that tree for a while, because he looked kind of sick. I told him to hold on and shimmied up the tree and cut the rope from his hands and his chest with my knife. There must've been a lot of dead leaves underneath because I don't remember any sound when he landed. It knocked the wind out of him anyway. He probably hadn't had much left. I stayed around to make sure he was okay, and he told me his own uncle did that to him. "Why?" I asked. He said he didn't know. "Tell your daddy on him," I said. "Pa's on a drunk," he answered, or something like that. He said they

10

lived in the coal camp at the foot of Shady Hollow, which my pappy had told me never to go near, though he didn't say why. Fergus gave me a big blue bead that he'd found in the old cemetery in Shady Hollow. I told him to come home with me and eat supper, and he did. I don't know what Pappy and Momma thought about it, but they fed him after Drue took him to the wash pan on the back porch and cleaned his face and hands. I told Momma where I found him and she took over from Drue and washed his chest and back and put salve on his rope burns.

After that, almost every school day Fergus would wait for me up on the hill—even in the snow—and walk home with me and get himself some supper. Well, he was only seven at the beginning, and I was just eight myself. My brothers were older than me and the other school kids lived too far away for much visiting. So I was buddies with Fergus. I found something... well, I guess I'd call it glamorous now, in his anger and in the way he talked about his folks as if they were younger than him. I've still got that blue bead, put away in the cigar box where I keep things I don't want to lose. I always obeyed my pappy about not going to Shady Hollow, though. It was easy, because Fergus didn't want me to go there either.

Although I was a little older, Fergus was the leader. At first we played settlers and Indians. Fergus always wanted to be an Indian but he would insist on winning half the time. "But the Indians *lost*," I would say, and he would answer, "How do you know? Was you there?" "Look around here," I said. "You see any Indians?" And he would say, "Yeah, *me*." It was exciting that he wanted to be an Indian. None of the other kids did, because the Indians always lost. Kinda like having a real enemy, one who would go home with you and eat supper.

When we reached around ten and eleven, we got up to some things like stealing Em Baker's pies off the windowsill where she had them cooling. Just orneriness. In my thirteenth year, Fergus's other uncle on his pa's side asked him to deliver some bootleg liquor. That was after Fergus's pa got killed in the mines, electrocuted. I overheard my pappy telling Momma Fergus's pa had been drinking. The uncle had an old wagon and a pair of broke-down old horses. We delivered the moonshine on Saturday in broad daylight. "Better that way," Fergus's uncle said. "Nobody'd suspect one of John Caskill's boys and in broad daylight." After our first delivery was successful, he asked us if we wanted to do it again, and he handed us a five-dollar bill apiece. So I got to know what's what about a lot of people in Osier County. We ran into Pappy once and told him we were hauling off some junk for Fergus's uncle. It was nearly a year before somebody told him the truth. That was the last whopping I got from him and it was a jim-dandy. Couldn't sit down good for a week. "Well," I'd said to him, "I don't see what's wrong with it. Even one of the preachers is buying."

"You ever see Ed Lander's wife after he's punched her good a time or two? Or Wally Dieters blind drunk and getting fired from his job loading coal? As for preachers, every bunch of men's got some bad apples. Don't prove nothing." Then he walloped me.

Momma was crying. "What if you get caught and land in jail?" she asked. "I know two deputies," I started, but Pappy hit me harder. After that, he kept me pretty busy at other things on Saturdays for a long time. He still let me play ball on school afternoons, though, and when I came home later, long after the others, Fergus would be waiting for me about halfway up the hill and he'd tell me about his deliveries and about goings-on in the county, goings-on that church people didn't talk about in front of their kids. I'd see some of the men I used to deliver to in church on Sunday, but they never let on that they knew me except as John Caskill's son. Their sons played ball with me, however, and some became my buddies in that way that boys—and men—have. Not buddy-buddy like Fergus and me.

After Pappy finally let up, Fergus and me got together a lot of Sunday afternoons and went fishing or hunting or, once in a while, to the train depot, where Fergus and older boys that he knew went to play poker. Their daddies played there on Saturday nights. Fergus would lend me a buck or two and I'd play until I ran out of money or time. If I won, I'd always pay Fergus back for then and for the other times. I had the feeling that I mustn't be beholden to Fergus, a feeling I've got up to this day. He's always had more money than me, for reasons I don't always know about or want to know about. Before Pappy found out about the bootleg deliveries, Fergus and me told each other peart nigh everything. But afterward I grew feelings toward things that I didn't share with him and I knew from others that Fergus got up to things he didn't tell me about. But there were things he did tell me about, about bootlegging and night trips and girls. They call me a good man, but I am bound to Fergus more than to any other man, and not just because I found him hanging from a tree, though that's part of it, and the fact that he treats me like a brother, that's part of it, and the years that lie behind us, that's part of it, and yet there is something left over, something that maybe I don't want to think about too much myself.

Fergus discovered girls a good while before I did. Well, I paid attention to them from a distance. Pappy took me above the flat, up where the land was almost dark with timber, I must've been about sixteen, and he said, "I don't want to hear of you getting a girl into trouble, if you know what I mean." Fergus had filled me in on the details, so I told him I knew. "And I know you're still buddies with Fergus Merritt," he said, with a dislike in his voice, though he never said anything when Fergus came to visit—probably figured it was best to have everything out in the open—"and I don't want to ever hear of you going around with the girls in that bunch."

"Ain't I supposed to even go near girls, then?" I asked. I was mad. Pappy throwing his weight around again—I thought

I was too big for that.

"Yeah, you are," he answered. "Just make it the right kind of girl and treat her right." But when I went near girls, I wanted to do things with them that I figured Pappy and the preachers wouldn't like.

Then I got that job loading coal in the Finley mine the week after I graduated high school. We did it without machines. Used the shovel and the back. There were three of us that buddied up in the mine, and we used to bet who'd load the most coal that day. It was dark and cold down there. Two men got killed in a rock fall, and there was talk of pockets of gas. I was glad when Pappy elected me to work in the store. By this time, I didn't see much of Fergus, and when we did get together we just went fishing or hunting. He did all his wild living with other people. I asked him once, just curious, why he didn't invite me in on some of his business, and he looked hard at me and said, "You wouldn't like it, and neither would I." So that's the way it's been with Fergus and me. I didn't have a girl yet, so I was saving money. Pappy and Momma were glad to have me at home.

Sometimes still Fergus came home with me, and he cottoned to Drue as much as to me. I don't know of any other woman he's treated like that. I was afraid Drue would fall for him, even though she was a few years older, and there were times I knew he'd come courting. I didn't want her to have anything to do with him, not in that way. Anyhow, it didn't matter, because Drue just treated him like a bird with a broken wing.

***

Drue used to wander off by herself all over these hills. Seems like it was safe for women to do that back then. I don't know why. There were sure men around who treated women bad. Men like Fergus, for one. I remember the day she killed herself as clear as anything. It was Saturday, and Pappy and I were fixing the fence around the pig lot. We had three fat ones, a boar and two sows. Pappy aimed to kill one of the sows come November. It was a hot August day, and you could see the heat shimmering out there. The barn had a tin roof, and I remember thinking that it would be hell to touch on such a hot day. Drue didn't give us any warning. I'd played checkers with her the night before, and she seemed about like usual. She was a sweet girl, with big brown eyes and her hair hanging loose. She never pulled it back in a bun the way Momma did. I can't remember her having a beau. When we were in school, there was a boy I teased her about, but I don't think she cared for him. Or maybe she did. After she graduated from school, well, then she did what other unmarried girls did. She stayed at home and helped Momma. She was real bright in school. It was over an hour after she jumped that the Willises found her.

***

So when the draft notice came, I had other things on my mind and wasn't expecting it. But I soon got fired up by the notion of traveling out there—hell, maybe across the Atlantic Ocean— and pretty damn scared. They didn't give me much time before they shipped me off to Texas. A lot of us Kentuckians down there, which was a good thing because some of the others wanted to make fun of our hillbilly accents. Couldn't make out who they hated more, us or the Mexicans. I liked the Mexicans, what I saw of them. I liked their food and I liked the way they had with colors and I liked the way they didn't let being in a strange place get them down or at least it didn't seem to.

I don't look back on the army with pleasure. Just the satisfaction of knowing I could do it and do it good. Fell in with California. Never knew his real first name. Him and me in that whorehouse. What I done there Pappy would have whipped the living daylights out of me for. She wasn't pretty. She was hard, hard covered up with red lipstick and red rouge. Well, if I'd had her life, I would have been hard, too. Maybe I was. The army was doing its best to teach me to be hard. I don't take no pleasure in that, either.

Anzio. Blood and pieces of people. I was still seasick, or maybe it was warsick. We didn't have enough ammo that week when California bought it. One of his legs way over to the right. He'd just finished pulling me up the riverbank. I thought maybe he'd say something like in the books, call for "Mommy" or "Daddy." But he was already dead. Sand in my gun. The Germans were right there. Some of them I killed were young boys. Swore I'd never hunt again, but I do. Dead men, pieces of meat. The shelters we put together underground. We made them out of anything we could find. Only place free of Jerry's guns. That Italian's wine cellar. I couldn't take it down there too long. Made me think of the mines. Hard to breathe. Thousands of us dead, they said. Felt sorry for myself because I didn't have a girl to write to. So I wrote to Pappy and Momma. She kept all the letters. I read them the summer after her death. It was over a hundred degrees that day. Sat there by her bed. I could feel her there as I read my letters. They didn't say much. What do you say to your folks about being in a war?

I did mention Rosa, though. Never forget that woman. Well, I probably won't have much longer to remember her. She'll have to depend on being remembered by her son's children. He had been hiding out from Jerry. A lot of Romans hid out from the Germans. They had surrendered and that probably made the Boches madder. Took everything that wasn't nailed down. The Eyeties were starving. Buildings boarded up. Even statues boarded up. Just my luck, I thought then, my first big city and one straight out of the history book and it's a war. Well, I did see the Colosseum and the outside of St. Peter's before I got wounded. Not in a fight; in a post office. Germans had set the explosives before they left town. In a post office sending a letter home.

Rosa couldn't have took better care of me if I was her own son. I wrote her a letter after I got home, a long letter telling her about all my kin and the hills and the store, but I never got an answer. Maybe her life was just too sad then. Maybe something happened to Paolo. Maybe she never got the letter. I'll never know. Every now and then I have a dream about Italy. Mostly they are bad dreams about the dead and the dying, but once or twice, once just last week, I've dreamed about Rosa's kitchen—the shiny stove with the blue flowers on it and that small table in the corner. Rosa is sitting across from me, ladling out some of her soup, and we are laughing. Rosa laughed a lot. Sometimes Joe Warshawski's wife will laugh in a certain way, with that accent of hers, and I am reminded of Rosa.

Joe and Lila came over here after the war. Until he retired, Lila always worried about Joe working in the mines. He had been a dentist in Poland. I asked him once what the war was like for him. Stupid question. He muttered something. "Don't you get homesick?" I asked. He got that far-off considering look people get when something big's at stake. "They're all dead," he said and walked out of the store without another word. I know Lila gets homesick. She still talks about their town and the people she knew there. Always before the war. Her uncle had a store.

After the war, I never had a hankering to ride on water in anything bigger than a canoe. A canoe on Lake Cumberland on a peaceful day. Jeff and me that summer after he graduated from high school. Half the fun watching my son enjoying being grown up. There were round rocks, like big balls, some of them burst open, with pieces like colored glass on the inside, shining in the sun. Geodes. Jeff had looked them up in some book in the school library. It was a kind of magic, the shining rocks and the lake as calm as Sarah Beth's mirror and my son catching almost as much fish as I did. We built us a fire and fried them right there by the lake. Almost dark by then. By the time we got on the road, the moon was high. Jeff pestered me to let him drive and then he fell asleep. Seems like it was the last time we were nice and easy like that. After that he was busy really growing up.

***

When I got back from the war, Pete had moved to Detroit to help build tanks, and he was staying on to work at the Ford plant. Bryan, too. Bryan had already married a Michigan woman. Susan and her man had moved to Ohio. Darryl had bought himself that bottomland where God's garden is and married one of the Hallem girls. (That summer Darryl and Tilda invited me over for supper once a week, and I hoped Darryl and me would get closer even though he was ten years older than me. But at that time he couldn't think about anything but his farm and Tilda, who I could see was expecting.) Momma was sick. Pappy had quit talking to everybody. He didn't even talk with his customers anymore beyond the necessary.

Some days my head felt like a hollow tree and I carried a silence around with me. I could forget it for a while talking to our customers, so I sort of took up with them where Pappy left off. One day after I'd been back a month or maybe two, Fergus walked into the store. "Well, it don't look like they messed you up too much," he said, smiling at me and cocking his left eyebrow in that way he has. I might not have looked different but I sure as hell felt different. Fergus didn't look a day older. Nothing touches him. Even now, the women, the ones who don't know him well, look and then look again. Sarah Beth can't stand the sight of him. She don't say anything but draws back like a snail withdrawing into its house.

I was glad to see him. I didn't particularly mean to be, and I hadn't gone looking for him because I knew he was no good.

He was no good in the way the hopeless are no good. With Fergus I always feel free to curse and speak my mind. Except we don't talk about our families. And now we don't talk about my death, because Fergus practically ran away when I brought the subject up. Back then I told him about the war, about Anzio and all those dead boys and pieces of boys. It was like he understood it all. Except Rosa. I didn't tell him about Rosa. Not really. I mentioned her, and he said, "Did you stick her?"

***

Girls—or, as Melissa wants me to say, women—came into the store too, of course. If Pappy was there, I didn't talk to them too much, but when he was gone, I found myself getting along pretty well. Sarah Beth would come in and I'd sit up and take notice. Her daddy was one of the preachers at our church and got on good with Pappy. Her cousin Sam and me used to play on the same ball team at school. I won't say that it wasn't part of why I liked Sarah Beth that her family went back to the American Revolution and was well respected. "I want a box of oats and a five-pound bag of sugar, and don't give me any of your sass, Orson Caskill," she might say. Mainly I favored her big brown eyes and the way her body always seemed to do whatever she wanted it to and the fact that she would sass me when I teased her. Which I liked to do.

Then there was that day Darcy Anne Titwell came into the store with a friend she was visiting, one of the Murphy girls. Darcy Anne's family didn't trade at the store. Oh no, they bought their groceries in town. Her granddaddy was part owner of the Duford Savings and Loan and lived in a big brick house on the edge of town. Her daddy was long gone from the hills, and every once in a while somebody still brought that story up. Some said he left because of Mrs. Titwell, who everybody knew was stuck up. She was a good teacher but we all knew she felt too good for the likes of us.

Darcy Anne, Mrs. Titwell the teacher's daughter. A good-looking girl, prettier than Sarah Beth, with blue eyes and red hair, and she was smart as a whip. Always won the spelling bees. Mrs. Titwell made sure that Darcy Anne read her book reports out loud, but Darcy Anne didn't like it much, you could tell. I don't suppose I'd ever exchanged more than a hundred words with her at school.

She came into the store and all of a sudden we were looking at each other and not paying attention to what Jeanie Murphy was saying. It wasn't that I forgot that I favored Sarah Beth. It was fever. After they left, Darcy Anne came back alone and bought a candy bar. I said, "It sure is pretty weather. Why don't you meet me out by the mill pond after supper?" Everybody knew what happened on moonlit nights at the mill pond, even me, though I'd never had reason to check it out. She answered, "Yes, yes, I will." Not another word more, except we fixed up the time. It wasn't that I felt like marrying Darcy Anne, which was what I'd been dreaming about with Sarah Beth. It wasn't like that at all, and I thought she felt the same way about it, the way she just went right ahead and met me that evening. But it turned out she didn't.

Well, now she's a hotshot professor up there in Chicago and my granddaughter is turning in work to her. Melissa likes her. I did too, all those years ago, after I got to know her. She's a straight shooter and it don't hurt her none with me that she hasn't forgot where home is, that she comes back here most summers and trades in the store. What I've got in mind this summer where she's concerned, I don't know if I should ask her. I don't know that I've got the right to ask it of her. But I've already made up my mind, I guess. The die is cast.

One thing was for sure: we neither one wanted anybody else to know about us getting together way back then. With me it was Pappy and Momma and the way they felt about carrying on outside marriage. And it was Sarah Beth. With Darcy Anne, well, I guess she was scared of Mrs. Titwell and maybe mixed in there too was that Titwell feeling of being too precious. She was sweet, Darcy Anne, younger than she looked with her hair all done up and wearing town clothes. When she told me she was going to have a baby, I was going to marry her. "Do you really want to?" she asked, looking straight at me. I kissed her so she couldn't see my face and said I did. Then she disappeared. After two or three weeks, I saw her by chance one day walking along the railroad tracks. Looking pale and crazy. I asked her where she'd been. "I lost the baby," she said, and the way she said it I wondered just how she had lost it. There were stories about this doctor in town. When Darcy Anne's mother sent her off to some college in Ohio, I felt sorry for her, but I was relieved. Oh, how I was relieved. She hadn't been gone more than a month before I asked Sarah Beth to go with me to see the circus that was in town. I couldn't wait any longer. Charley Murphy was courting her. My mother liked Sarah Beth. She got along good with Sarah Beth's ma, and Sarah Beth would stand there after church and talk to them about the weather and the crops and the general way of things.

Momma was the person in this world I loved most. It wasn't that she was what you'd call a good woman. Well, she was. She didn't pay much attention to the needs of anybody else, but she would do anything for her family. My earliest picture of her, she's bent over that washboard, her hands rubbing up and down, up and down, up and down. She heated the water outside, that old black tub perched on two columns of rock. She canned in that tub, too, and if I'm not bad mistaken, used it for making the lye soap, and to heat water for the pig killings. She had two shiny galvanized tubs for washing clothes. Taking a bath in a round, galvanized tub by the kitchen stove. The front of me burning a little and my backside freezing. Afterward Pappy and Darryl or maybe Pete and Bryan would cart the water and dump it out in the garden. Never seemed to hurt any.

I think Momma only went to church because she thought

21

it was good for the family. You never saw her reading the Bible. She had a few books, stories, and she would read them over and over. I liked *The Tale of Two Cities* best. Well, she also went to church because of Pappy. She wouldn't stand up against Pappy for what she considered little matters. That was something she saved for important occasions, like the time Pappy was going to throw Darryl out. I was pretty young at the time, maybe eight, maybe nine. I heard the strikes of Pappy's razor strop. Darryl never said a word. He never told me what he had done, either, and I don't know to this day. But I heard the way Momma and Pappy threw words at each other. Scared me half to death to hear Momma carrying on like that. She was a small woman with her black hair pulled back in a bun, her head cocked a little bit to one side when she looked at you and found you good, and mostly she didn't raise her voice. Darryl got off with a good licking. He was almost as big as Pappy, but he just took what I guess was coming to him.

Momma's biscuits light as air, even lighter than Sarah Beth's, and her cobblers just right, not too sweet but sweet enough. She was a good cook and a good cleaner and good in the garden and a good listener. You could tell Momma anything so long as it didn't have anything to do with sex. I didn't tell her about the war, though, because I didn't want her to know the kind of man I'd been. The killing, the whoring. The main reason I didn't want her to know was for me. Momma put a certain trust in me, which my friendship with Fergus didn't spoil because she knew I didn't do the things people told her Fergus did. That trust was like a balm for me when I got back. It let me keep the boy I had been and go forward.

So I took Sarah Beth to the circus. I'd been once before, when I was a boy. My nose perked up at the smell of sawdust and animals. Swirls of color. I preferred the horses and Sarah Beth loved the trapeze act. Afterward, both of us keyed up, I took her home in that crazy old Ford I had and dawdled a while on her front porch, knowing better than to kiss her, but

I did, for the first time. She pressed against me. It was a fine summer night, white stars all over the deep blue dusk and the sound of tree frogs smoothing out the evening and letting it flow with me as I left her and made my way home to Sarvis Mountain.

Pappy was sitting on the porch, and Darryl was there and had his arms around Pappy, something I had never seen nor ever would again. Momma had choked on something, just a bite of everyday food. She was already dead when Pappy went into the kitchen to see what was holding supper up. Didn't get to say goodbye. We buried her in the Caskill graveyard on the other side of the mountain, right beside Drue, and I felt they were lonely there, shut off from the rest of us.

All the people around me had faith but I did not. When Momma died, I figured she was just that—dead. Her body a piece of meat in the white pine coffin. Nobody I knew, but still I thought she must be lonely.

I'm trying to get faith now, for Sarah Beth and for me, mainly for me. I wish for a different kind of church. Maybe if I'd been a Catholic and went to church in St. Peter's, it would've been another matter. Too late now. Too late for that but if I take my mood at God's pond and run with it, I come upon something like hope.

After Momma died, Pappy just gave up. Pretty much turned the store over to me right then. I'd come home in the evening and he'd be sitting on the front porch rain or shine, even after it started getting cold. After the first snow fell, he'd be sitting at the kitchen table, with the Bible open in front of him, that considering look in his eyes. I'd try to get him talking about the store but he'd say a word or two and go silent again. He'd have supper ready and waiting for me on the stove. Too many pinto beans. Pappy couldn't cook worth a damn. He was grieving over me because I didn't go to church anymore. But I didn't give him that. It seemed so important then not to. Now I've done it out of love for Sarah Beth. No god I'd care about would mind. Who knows, maybe wouldn't mind about Fergus either. I've been a good in Fergus's life, I believe. And maybe Fergus has taken on himself all the evil I might have done. Not all of it, that's for sure, but something like that.

***

The first time I cheated on Sarah Beth was right before Charlene was born. My cheating didn't have anything to do with my wife and my baby is the way I felt. Sarah Beth and me had stopped getting together. Her thoughts were on that baby. I thought about the baby, too, but more about whether Sarah Beth would be okay.

Anyhow, I took that run over to Saddle Creek to see Uncle Henry and Aunt Matilda—both long dead now. Uncle Henry was Pappy's favorite brother and just as like him as peas in a pod, religion and everything. He made me jumpy but I loved him, seeing Pappy in him even in the way he was loving to Matilda. Jeff is like that, too—the wife part. I don't think he believes much more in religion than I do, but I could be wrong.

Of course they fed me. It was two o'clock in the afternoon and I already ate dinner before I set out, but they had to feed me. I overheard one of Char's boys say when they were little and Char and that husband of hers were taking them to see a string of kinfolk, "Do we have to eat this time, too?" We're like that in the hills. Maybe it's because so many of us have known one time or another when we didn't have enough to eat. Not me or Sarah Beth after we got married. We had the store. Well, excepting that one year in the fifties. I remember that winter when the mines went bust and nobody was coming into the store to speak of. I came near to closing, and we didn't have any meat practically all that winter. We only had the one rooster and the laying hens. I did kill one hen for Christmas dinner. And we had eggs and the cannings out of the garden, but our kin didn't all have land, and we gave a lot of the canned food to some of them, the ones who were hurting the most. Along about March, it was pretty lean pickings. I was put in mind of my boyhood.

So Matilda heated up this and that and fried some pork while I sat down and chewed another kind of fat with Henry. He quoted Scripture at me here and there and asked me did I go to meeting last Sunday but other than that it was okay. It was getting late when I left, though still a long way from dark and still that July heat. I stopped my old Chevy at Gracie Lake, which was in them days a real pretty place and jumping with fish. Mine runoff has ruint it now. And there she was, old Amos Hallem's girl May Ellen, sitting on a rock and ready and willing. Men talked about her. Fergus hadn't been there, though. I wouldn't have touched her if she had been with Fergus. Our lives never ran together that way. A soft girl on a hard rock. I like May Ellen. She got married at last to Jonas Murphy and she's been true to him as far as I know. They've got three grown sons and I don't know how many grandkids.

Swore I never would cheat again, and I didn't until Tessie was a baby and I took up with Venetta. Venetta's mother was second cousin to Sarah Beth, and that makes it worse. And her uncle drove the Royal Crown Cola truck, and I used to stop when I was out that way and sit on his front porch talking politics. He was a Republican, and that made it interesting. Us Democrats always used to be in the majority around here. Anyhow, one time when I stopped back then, Venetta's uncle and his wife were out, and Venetta was next door or so watching her other aunt's children. I had Tessie with me, and Venetta fussed over her and laughed with me and at me. Before I knew it, we were exchanging that kind of look. One of her eyes was gray and the other one sky-blue, and her copper hair was on fire. I'm a sucker for women with spirit—and, sometimes I guess, red hair.

From then on I made sure I left the children at home. Until that time I was careless and took Jeff and he looked in the window. I always wanted to know how much he guessed. Not that we were doing anything by then. I saw her maybe three times a year for about five years. Then we stopped. A distance had come between me and Sarah Beth and I knew that was the reason, and finally Sarah Beth caught on.

Venetta wanted someone to marry. I know for a fact, though, that Charlie Alseck asked her and she turned him down. We stayed good friends. Sarah Beth doesn't know that.

So these two women and Darcy Anne I've held out on my wife about, though she found out something about Venetta. I don't reckon there's anything else about me she don't know. Except why I'm friends with Fergus. Except that I'm a Woodrow. Good lord. She might have called me Woody. We almost split up once when we were still young, before Char was born, but it wasn't over other women. I had got in the habit of going over to the depot and playing poker on Saturday nights. I was losing money and coming home more than a little drunk. One night I treated her rough when she sassed me. The next morning she went back to her parents. She wouldn't look at me. I was shamed, too. It was bad. It was like going away from home. Like losing the whole state of Kentucky. I forced myself to tell her I was ashamed of myself, and I promised to quit drinking more than a whiskey or two at a time, and I promised to quit playing for money. And I've kept those promises, too, except for the penny ante games I used to play with the children. I'd pretend to cheat, all the while letting them win, at least 'til they got bigger, and they'd pretend they thought I was cheating.

Potatoes roasting under the grate, maybe, or popcorn popping in Sarah Beth's big iron skillet. Little hands stretching out to hold the cards, all of them as fixed on the game as any gambler. It's a wonder none of them grew up to be card sharps. Jeff and Char still get that devil look in their eyes when somebody mentions playing cards. Tessie's got her mind on other things. Tessie's more like her mother, even to that long brown hair and big brown eyes. They find life satisfying enough as it is. Tessie always played with whatever toys she had in front of her, but Jeff and Char looked around for something else, like as not something that Tessie was playing with.

Their mother read to them from the time they were three. The first books she got off a rack at Western Auto, Little Golden Books. (Sitting on the back porch on a summer afternoon, just before the twilight came, her smooth brown head bent over the book and over the children, Tessie sitting on her lap, Char on a neighbor chair, Jeff on the floor, the velvet sound of her voice.) Sometimes I read to them, too, but Sarah Beth did it practically every day. As they grew older and the books became things like *Treasure Island*, I used to listen too sometimes. We had a family make-believe about Long John Silver and his parrot (I was Long John, of course). Jeff always goes to Sarah Beth about books. And Jeff and Char and Tessie all used to listen to the children's radio shows, drinking Pepsis with peanuts in them. Mostly out of Nashville. I read history and westerns, like I always did, but Sarah Beth reads anything, and she's the one that likes to keep the books all neat and in a row, so I made her the bookshelves. I laugh when Melissa calls it our library, but Sarah Beth likes it. All them books on Kentucky she has.

Momma didn't have many books to read but she knew the ones she had backward and forward. Pappy never read anything but the Bible. The Alsecks, Sarah Beth's family, had schoolteachers—Albert and Lavinia, both dead now. My children never knew their Caskill grandparents. Pappy and Momma both dead before Charlene was born. Jeff's wife's family looks down on the Caskills and thinks she married beneath her. Hell, her grandparents spend most of their time in Lexington. They only came down here because he took over old Doc Williams's patients.

Things about people I know that I learned just working in the store. The loneliness of old men and women coming into the store every afternoon, meeting to gab, killing time before going back to that shack up the holler where there's not enough to eat now (a lot of times they don't buy a thing when they come in) because they got to buy medicine, wife or husband dead, children scattered across the earth. Because there's never enough work anymore, and some people go hungry. I can't give them all credit, the mines going bust again. The younger men who can't find mine jobs maybe working on them goddamn roads they're building all over the place now.

Most of us try to draw a line around our little green pockets of earth and say "It won't happen here" where the folks still come to Sunday dinner. Trying not to pay too much attention to Cousin Audry's drinking habit or the cancers the Tibbett family may be getting because of the bad water in their well or the ugly scar above the house where the water gathers and there'll be a mudslide one of these days and maybe a little girl will wander into one of the abandoned mines that nobody knows where it goes.

Every place around us full of ghosts who call to us and dirt and trees and rocks that call to us.

Have I ever told my son that I'm proud of him? We get along fine except for Fergus. I know Jeff despises him and despises his daddy too in that regard, oh yes, he does, even though all I ever do with Fergus is a little hunting and fishing and a Saturday drink or two. If I told Jeff about Darcy Anne, would he despise her, too, for his mother's sake? I wonder if Darcy Anne told Sarah Beth something while I was in the hospital because Sarah Beth turns away when she sees her and she said to me once after church, after Darcy Anne had nodded at us, when we were on the way home alone on that day, me looking out at a spring day and seeing the trees flying beneath the sun, on their way to my death. It was all green that Sunday and the blue sky flying above carrying the sun. Sarah Beth driving in that slow, awkward way she has, having come to it only after I got sick, bent over the steering wheel 'til you would think she wasn't looking ahead. She said to me, "I don't know you, all these years and I don't know you." I must have looked at her kind of pitiful because she gave me a quick look and laughed a little and said, "But I like the part I know." If I hadn't been sick, we'd have had a big fight right there. She won't fight with me anymore. I miss that.

And the children. They're all too nice to me now. That time when Char graduated from high school and I wouldn't let her go to town with that bunch of boys her boyfriend hung around with. She sassed me and she wouldn't stop. I shouted at her and she went out onto the back porch and cried. I'd seen them boys in town, at the Crystal Inn, high on something and it wasn't beer or whiskey because they weren't drinking. I never liked that Curtis boy anyhow. Like his dad, loud-mouthed and lazy. Anyway, that ended when she went to UK. But look who she took up with there. Poor Char, she always takes things hard, not like Jeff or Tessie.

It took a load off my mind when Jeff married Bernice, but I hope he don't let her talk him right out of Kentucky. And Tessie's Floyd is a decent, hardworking man. I hate it that they're so poor right now. Me and Sarah Beth offered to help them out some, but Floyd said no. My children. Jeff's close with Tessie, and Char is close with Tessie, but I see that Jeff and Char don't always hit it off so good. Tessie's like her mother. Char reminds me of my side of the family. Jeff, he's a hybrid. I see now that he should've gone to college like Char. But not UK, no, the one in town.

***

Well, Jervis Alseck's on his feet now, ready to help these kids tie the knot. Jervis is a reasonable man and never shouts his preaching out like our souls are deaf and never says that anybody who don't belong to this church is in for hellfire and damnation. He just says everybody ought to treat their neighbor right. *But that on good ground are they which in an honest and good heart, having heard the word, keep it, and bring forth fruit with patience.* The bride and groom look to me like children playing dress-up, Emile in his good gray suit and Bertha all gussied up in white satin, but wildflowers in her hand. I used to hold Emile's father on my knee.

I'm going to talk to Sarah Beth about a family reunion, my family, before the summer is over. Susan is talking about coming down from Ohio, because of my sickness I know, but that's all right. Maybe some of her kids and Peter's kids will come if we talk reunion, and poor Bryan's wife and daughter. He was electrocuted on the job. I picture my brother like a wild man in the comic books, his hair sticking out with electricity and his arms and legs stiff and wide and a look on his face like he was holding back a bushel of laughter. He liked to laugh, my brother Bryan. He looked the most like Pappy, but he wasn't natured like him. Darryl's Lily will come over, bringing the world's best banana pudding.

I picture them, my first family, at suppertime, sitting around that table Pappy made of oak he cut and seasoned and planed himself. It's high summer and there's green beans and tomatoes and watermelon for dessert. Before I went to school. Momma a young woman dishing out the beans and Bryan making us laugh. Pappy said grace, of course, and Pete reached for the cornbread. Pete was crazy about cornbread and butter. Well, I like 'em pretty good myself. Probably everybody but Momma and Susan had spent the day back in the cove hoeing corn. Susan bringing us biscuits and sausage and maybe some cold spicewood tea.

A great satisfaction I always took has been going into the woods and finding the spicewood bushes, breaking off the sweet-smelling twigs, bringing an armful home for Sarah Beth to pile in the kettle and add the water and put on the stove. Tastes a lot better than sassafras tea. Or gathering ground ivy for the babies and making enough tea for the grownups to have a half-cup or so. And catnip. But my favorite is spice-wood.

Pappy's hair was still brown and he had been teaching me how to hoe the corn, how you can only do so much with the hoe and then you have to bend down and pull out the weeds near the corn and then heap the fresh dirt around it but not to make a ditch. He was patient about it, like Pappy always was about work—though, Lord knows, not about other things.

Once him and me went walking in the new snow up in the mountains, just the two of us. Maybe the rest were at school, except Drue, who was probably home with Momma. Just the two of us, and we're investigating tracks in the snow. We come up over a rise and down below us in the valley were hundreds of redbirds, red against the snow and the bite of the cold on my hands and both of us quiet, watching the birds. When I was that young boy, I thought the sun rose and set with my Pappy.

When we found out Sarah Beth was pregnant that first time, we decided to take a honeymoon. It was not long before Pappy died and he was sickly, but he said he'd watch over the store. Well, we didn't call it a honeymoon at the time. Just a real trip, the first such for us; if we left the house it was either to go get something in town or to visit family or to keep a doctor's appointment. Cars were slower then and roads were worse. We decided to go to Lexington, because Sarah Beth was curious what the city was like since she'd only been to the hospital there to see her Pa before he died, and she wanted to know what Bluegrass looked like.

I felt kind of in danger once we reached as far north as that beautiful farmland around the city. No hills. But it was like getting drunk, too, all the open farmland and the brick houses with their white columns. And the horses. We didn't have television then. (Jeff was practically out of high school when we got that seventeen-inch black and white TV. I wonder if my children remember how we all liked Sid Caesar. That show where he kept saying he gotta get couth. Sarah Beth is couth, because she just is, and Tessie, but the rest of us are trying to get there.)

When Sarah Beth and I got to downtown Lexington, we both felt uncouth, though. I can tell you that. The fine houses and the stores and all the people. I was sure I was going to bump into somebody while we made our way here and there looking for a hotel. We found one right in the middle of town, a fine place with red plush chairs in the lobby and shiny bathrooms. The people weren't dressed like us. I mean, we both had on new clothes, but my shirt didn't have proper cuffs and Sarah Beth's dress was way too long. And they didn't talk like us; they talked like teachers and the sound was softer and more tuneful. Well, not all of them. For instance, there were some of us in town, clerking behind the desk in the lobby, waiting on people in the restaurants. I guess you could say that put Sarah Beth and me in our place. Some of the people we asked directions from wouldn't look at us but others were as nice as pie and proud of the place.

Sarah Beth bought a dress in this big place right in the middle of town, one of those that have everything, from clothes to furniture to refrigerators. I took her in there and waited while she chose a soft green dress. She was flushed and pretty. She said she could wear it and then put it away until after the baby was born. In the evening, we went to a place where they had music that the hotel clerk told us about. They were playing what he told us was jazz, as of course I know now. I liked it and the way they played it. Made me feel loose and easy and like kissing Sarah Beth, which I did right out there in public, not that we were the only ones kissing. Sarah Beth pretended to be scandalized. We were young. Sarah Beth wearing that soft green dress.

We spent one more day and night and by then we were ready to head home, and we got lost in all that open land. Took us two extra hours to find ourselves and be on our way. We had just enough money left to buy gas. We were lost together and we were young. We're lost again now, Sarah Beth and me.

Our soul is escaped as a bird out of the snare of the fowlers; the snare is broken, and we are escaped.

I have loved the snare.

DARCY

I sit here in this church, so familiar yet so far, watching my niece marry one of Orson's kin. I see Orson's eyes lingering on her. Is he thinking that Bertha looks a lot like I once looked? The red hair, the blue eyes, and the pale skin that used to show up in my mirror. That innocent thing. Though never was I innocent. It is just one huge room, this church, with its oak floor and oak window frames stained a darker brown. There are no pews, just benches really, and up front the platform with more benches, where the initiated sit—still men on one side, women on the other, and in the middle usually the preachers, plural, but today Jervis Alseck, who is marrying his second cousin to his affianced. We are not dressed in homespun as most of us were when I was a child, in the old church, although I see Granny Macomber in an ancient dress that was surely made from a feedsack once upon a time. Her father used to bank in my father's bank, coming in probably every few months to augment his painfully thin savings account, and her mother probably shopped in the Caskills' store. On impulse I catch Granny Macomber's eye and wave hello and though she may not remember who I am, still she nods in a friendly fashion as people will in Osier County.

Last week I was still in Chicago, still sitting in my office in the gray, block-like building that houses my department, a building so at variance with the Gothic crannies and spires of the main buildings on campus that I cringe on entering its dusty, uninspired corridors. They must have been saving money when they built it during the big war. Pennywise and foolish of spirit. Not that the Gothic buildings are beautiful, but they've got character.

Orson's granddaughter Melissa had just walked out. I am one of her dissertation advisers. She is enthusiastic because I am from her neck of the woods. Born and bred in the briar patch, Brer Fox, born and bred in the briar patch. We had been discussing *The Tempest*, which Melissa is managing to give a Kentucky accent. Her thinking on the hills is a few decades out of date, back to the time when some social historians wrote of eastern Kentucky as sheltering the noble woodsman and his family. Melissa, who is no fool, has updated the image to a conscious state of innocence such as the duke created around Miranda. I blue-pencil these purple passages each time she delivers another installment, but next time another avatar will crop up.

At first she tried to get personal information from me, along the lines of why did *I* leave the hills. She knows that her grandfather and I had some kind of a friendship. I wonder if Orson told her that. I like his granddaughter. In some ways we are alike, but she is a happier person than I am. She comes from a good family. The Caskills have been around the hills for a long time, and they are sound, I think. What would I have been like now if I had had a chance to marry Orson? Melissa comes home often, but I think she is conflicted about where her future lies.

When I return to Osier County in these short summers, more and more often I fold my hands softly, sitting on my sister Luellen's front porch, and let the hills encircle me. Green mountain shadow, blue sky, and the crystal creek down below where Luellen's grandchildren play half-clothed. Mountains are axes joining heaven and earth. Gods play there at sunrise, the Taoists say, and perfected beings fly there. In Taoist meditation, the inner human body is a mountain landscape, its forms simultaneously reflecting the natural world and the cosmos. Luellen's grandchildren are perfected beings, sun tangled in their hair and water sparkling in their hands, their opaque gazes focused on the flowing creek.

Mornings I get up at my sister's call and go milk the cow before breakfast. How surprised my Chicago students would be to find me here, in old jeans and my dead brother-in-law's shirt, my hair falling long and straggly instead of fashioned into a chignon by a more-than-competent hairdresser. It certainly makes Melissa nervous when she runs into me at the post office. Yesterday I twirled a rubber band around the hair and borrowed the car and went down to the Caskill grocery to buy a banana flip and a pint of milk for lunch and go into the deep woods.

There are certain days yet when someone else lives my life. She is the spirit of the girl I was, the shadow who grew up here while I was elsewhere. On those days, I envy Sarah Beth, Melissa's grandmother, whose daddy the preacher was a coal miner weekdays. My lost self doesn't resemble Sarah Beth, though, who is *not* lost in the woods never been good. On those lost days, I pick up where that unhappy teenager left off when she went north and I remember, among other things, my passion for Orson, Sarah Beth's husband. I remember my red-hot shame when I ran to him and he nodded and turned away. My former husband, my accomplice in that short, unhappy marriage north of the Mason-Dixon Line, has less reality to me than Orson does, though it's forty-five years since Orson's brown fingers unbuttoned my dress and I helped him, oh, yes, I helped him. The shiver of hair on the back of his hand.

I haven't been able entirely to shed her, this untaught girl who's been starving at the back of my mind for forty-five years, since the fall I went away to Brisson University and jump-started my new self, the one that bought her clothes at the most fashionable shop in town and went to the Methodist church, which was where my classmates went. Never to the little wooden Primitive Baptist church down on the rickety side of town, where the women with their untaught hair and the men with large, red, callused hands showed up on Sundays, coming out of rickety streets and talking their rickety talk. Even my father the banker had been such a Baptist.

Today I sit in Sarah Beth's church, not the plain wooden one that her father used to preach in but the new brick one, squat and efficient, and I look at Sarah Beth's great-grand-parents on the wall behind the members' platform just where they were in the old church and then at her cousin Jervis Alseck marrying Emile and Bertha. Jervis used to sit beside me in the fifth grade. His nose was always running then, but he had large gray eyes fringed with black lashes and he was a wiz at math. I outdid him in English and geography and history and it killed me that I never got anywhere near his level in arithmetic. Now he drives a school bus on weekdays and preaches on Sunday. His gray eyes acknowledge mystery as he gets up a good head of steam preaching-wise but he never tries to shout it out as some of the others do. Last July I accompanied Luellen and her grandchildren one Sunday and listened to him elaborate on Naomi and Ruth, trills of emotion clustering around his firm belief that these were two women who would have made good Kentucky neighbors. The foreign Naomi called to him from beyond the alien corn. She didn't, he said, let her difference keep her from loyalty to her husband's family, but shone like a star among familiar things, walking through the corn, perhaps, side by side with Ruth, pulling off roasting ears for the boys' dinner. A packsaddle got me once when I was helping one of my school friends pull corn. It had a funny little saddle on its woolly wormy back.

Felt like the devil's pinch. A demon devil, none of your bourgeois Mephistopheles who depend on reason, but a passionate red-hot fundamentalist devil who undoubtedly peeked at
Naomi and Ruth among the corn and chalked another one up
for God.

I did not cleave to my husband's family, or they to me. But
when I am in Chicago, I keep his name, as a blanket against the
cold. I remember 1950. We had been married for a year, and he
went to Europe for two months and left me behind with his
sister until he could figure out a decent way of ditching me
altogether, which was all right, because we were accomplices
in the matter. Sweet James Brant, who saved me from the law
and from Ken. James's father was a pottery manufacturer and
James was a sociology major with a sweet face and thin brown
hair, tall, vulnerable and thin and courageous of aspect. Now
and then I hear from him. He remarried long ago, to the girl
next door practically. She's from Cleveland, too, and they met
in sociology class. He had dropped her to rescue me. On the
rare occasion when I call James, she sometimes answers the
phone, and her voice goes cold. Sometimes their one grand-
child, whose family lives nearby, answers the phone.

In the silence that follows the wedding ceremony, I look at
Jervis Alseck's face—gathering itself for a preacherly finale, or
concentrating upon what has been, what is to come. Perhaps
that is as close to the authentic Jervis as I can get. Or, if not,
then in the idiosyncrasies of his sermons, the halting, delving
fervor that chooses one verb rather than another that, yes, fits
together, *structures* the received text.

We are all bundles of historical texts, religious texts, ethnic
texts, criminal texts, etcetera. One must listen to the silences
to be wise, and create silences, formal silences like those that
paint a Kentucky hillside as a Taoist text.

***

In my college days, I was sailing along on the surface of things at Brisson, ignoring the slow, dark mutter of my homeless soul and getting high on all-night talk in the dorm and on shards of poetry flung aside by professors and on my pretty dresses purchased, as I said, at the most fashionable shop in town. One night my roommate and I went to an off-limits party on the wrong side of town, and after I'd had two beers I found myself sitting in a dark corner with Ken. Ken was a former Brisson student who had quit after his sophomore year. He was a big, handsome boy with purple eyes and a dark beard. He talked long and passionately, quoting the *New York Times*, but scornfully. He was from Scarsdale. His father was a surgeon and his mother was what women always were in those days. (Though not *my* mother.) Ken wasn't talking to either of his parents. His anger called to my homeless, angry soul. I let him lead me to his one-room apartment on the wrong side of town and coax me into making love to him.

After we dynamited the real estate office (which belonged to the mayor—Ken said it was for practice and anyhow the mayor had snubbed him some time or other), I went on the run with him, but the police didn't know that. They thought they got the only girl when they found Jennifer hiding in the college gym. "I'm sick of your miserable whining face anyhow," Ken said. "If you didn't want to blow up anything, nobody made you."

"We blew *somebody* up."

"Don't exaggerate, Darcy. She just got a broken rib or two."

"She lost an arm."

"Just shut up, Darcy," he said, "and stay with James." I'd been hiding out with James, because James felt, in so many words, there but for the grace of God. James had belonged to our secret society for a while but he got out when Ken went crazy.

Sweet James, who had a scared, depressed young woman on his hands with straggling hair and stuttering speech, who suddenly didn't believe in anything, certainly not herself. James was spending his first year as a social worker in one of Cleveland's poorer districts, and all his tenderness went to his clients. He worked long after-hours and weekends, helping set up programs for the children. Sometimes when I am unhappy, I find my hand caressing something and I realize I'm caressing James, giving him the love I never did then. No, I had given myself to Ken, who took love as something that was his due.

***

I could talk more now of those years at college and of the later years in Columbus and Chicago, of Darcy Brant the pro-fessor. Doesn't my original name, Titwell in particular, sound like an anomaly? I cut out the "Anne" for a while and then I married James Brant of Shaker Heights, Ohio, right outside Cleveland. Doesn't that sound just about right? You might say the tale existed in the black hole where Titwell used to be. Too weighty and too trite in the telling and the journey there and back, a poem of luminous terror. They tend to forget about the "Brant" back here in Kentucky; as often as not, they still call me Mz. Titwell. Or Darcy Anne.

In my Kentucky summers, I get up early to milk the cow, her rough flank grazing my cheek as the warm milk steams into the aluminum bucket, while Luellen cooks breakfast and gets her grandchildren ready for school. Her eldest daughter left them here a year ago, when she got that teaching job in Johnson County. She comes home on the weekend. I drove over to Paintsville once to see her, and she was shacked up with one of the other teachers. If her ex-husband finds out about it, he'll try to get custody again. Janice Sue says her new man is going to marry her. I hope to God so. See, that's not me speaking. That's the one I left behind. But it won't do, all the same, for her ex to get custody. He's shaky and he drinks too much.

I told Luellen to turn off the television last night. They had caught up with a Weatherman who had gone in for violent protest during Vietnam. He now looked like an aging parody of a 1950s freshman. Ken had been tall and in good shape, his beard like a burst of midnight. His face suffered, but I didn't know it suffered only for himself. To be fair, neither did he. The arm of that woman lying in the dust. Flesh and blood stuck to her white blouse.

The first day I came to Brisson, my mother brought me, of course, only too ready to impose herself on the scene. *She* went to UK, but when I got the scholarship to Brisson, she said I had to take it, such a fine upstanding college where rich men sent their children. Luellen had done okay for herself by marrying Tom Hollis, the mining company's lawyer. Now it was my turn. But I'd almost had a baby out of wedlock, horrors. So I cried over Orson Caskill, who threw me over for Sarah Beth anyhow but why shouldn't he when my mother kept hawk watch on me and I never got to see him alone after that summer, that summer before she found out, and I left the town where nobody understood me, heigh-ho the dearie-o, and went to Brisson, where for survival's sake my life would be dedicated to understanding others—that is, staying one jump ahead.

Brisson was a pretty how town with up so many—really—floating bells down. There were ten churches in town, and five of them had bells. From one, I remember, on Saturday afternoon would float out songs like "Moonlight Bay" and "Barb'ry Allen." Young lovers would go to the brown bridge beneath the willows by the gray chapel and neck to the sounds of "Someone to Watch Over Me." Funny about songs. Music is the soul of nostalgia. It gets you whatever you may think of, say, Sinatra's philandering habits when he was off-key, so to speak. And Brisson had a lake to reflect the sound waves the bells made in the willow branches and beneath Sunday blue skies and among the white-columned red-brick homes of the faculty. The faculty was better than the school, the rag and tag of them from everywhere, Spain and Switzerland and France, Mississippi and Yale (which surely sounded like a whole state all to itself). I think they even had a Harvard guy or two. I wish I had been grown up enough to find out their stories. Some of them were nice to me, the girl from the hills with her long, untrimmed hair and her *I want I want I want.* (I loved *Henderson the Rain King* years later on.) Others were not so nice.

The first year, I followed my mother's plan and lived in a dormitory full of girls who had pairs of white gloves, but the girl next door was a Pakistani sophomore, Nadira, and she didn't seem to understand I was an outcast. She was not middle class like the others—well, like me, but you'd never have known it and by then I didn't either. I felt "hillbilly," not "banker's daughter." There's a lot in the nomination—her father was enormously wealthy, and she knew by now what it was like to be an outsider. She had the courage (and the financial reserves) to be one. So we became friends, or rather she befriended me, and we decided we'd room together and move into the local lepers' colony, a cooperative where girls who didn't belong to sororities lived.

***

The mines were booming when our father built the house where Luellen lives (it is half mine). I always think of him thus, formally, with a hint of rejected prayer. How old was I when he left us and went to California? About seven. I barely remember him. But I remember Mother well enough. I remember Mama. How much I should have liked, once, to call her Mama or Mommy or Ma. "I come from an old Virginia family." How many times did I hear her tell that lie? Her granddaddy was third cousin to the Virginia Pelhams, but he came to Kentucky dirt-poor and he didn't know any of his posh relatives. *My* grandfather, his son, said his daddy lived in a hollow tree the first winter. Then he made a fortune when the railroad came through. Nouveau riche, and newcomers, too. Sarah Beth Caskill, née Alseck, has a Revolutionary War colonel in her family.

The way Sarah looks at me when she politely says hello. That's our Sarah. That genteel circumspection is not all that rare here on Sarvis Creek. Not shabby-genteel, though God knows it's often shabby and it's genteel. My mother was the phony genteel around here.

***

Going into Osierville to visit Granddaddy Pelham, I didn't like that brick house because it was dark, and he was broken. Parkinson's disease, but all I saw was someone out of control. And she was gentle with him, my mother. He was the only man I ever saw her be sweet to. Schoolteacher Titwell, that was my mother. And she was good at it, yes, my mother was. Her students were half-scared of her and they mimicked her airs but they admired her and they learned from her.

A dirt road between our house and the schoolyard then. Hurrying to keep up with Mother in the mud, globs of it sticking to my shiny brown shoes. The smell of her old leather bookbag in the rain. One day, I fell, and she sent me back to change clothes and I ran into Fergus on the bridge. He grabbed my arm and twisted it and took my lunch. "If you tell, you'll be sorry." Then he kissed me. Everybody said how handsome he was. Could get any woman he wanted. They said. He always looked like the devil to me. That laughter in his eyes his secret work.

I loved the schoolhouse. "Did you really go to a one-room school?" my Chicago friends ask. The scarred old desk chairs and the cherry-bellied stove exactly at room's center. The recitation benches that Mother kept shining with Murphy's oil.

The time Mother whipped us. I wonder if Sarah remembers that. We went playing in the rain after she told us not to. Sarah cried, but I wouldn't. Mother made me go get the willow limb. I wouldn't give her the satisfaction of crying.

I was sorry for Simon Amfeldt. She kept him in the second grade year after year. He used to pull his pants down in the schoolyard sometimes. Probably had a mental age of about three. He didn't have food that day and I gave him half my sandwich, and they chanted, "Darcy's got a sweetheart." But I had friends. Jane Nestor—tawny-headed Jane, who kept cigarettes in her lunch bag. I wonder what happened to her. Her family moved away. Luellen told me that Jane's daddy used to sell votes out behind the church on Election Day.

Orson—he was my friend, too.

But Mother sent me to Osierville High School. Living in that dark house with Granddaddy and Sally, that was her name, that weird old woman who kept house for him and told me ghost stories on dark nights.

"Old man Simmons had been out to Sandy Jones's still and got hisself a skinful. On the way back he had to pass the Alsecks' graveyard. The moon was shining in and out of the clouds, and it being October it was kind of nippy. Old man Simmons was shivering by the graveyard fence when he seed this white light. 'You come on out here, boys,' he said. 'You ain't scarin' me none. I know it's some of you fool Vinner boys.' Nobody said a thing and the light got closer, and then closer, and then closer, and old man Simmons opened the gate to catch hold of one of them boys and a big old Indian took a blanket and dropped it over his head. He shook it off and ran like a turkey at Thanksgiving and the light ran after him until he fell down in a faint." ("Faint, my eye," his wife probably said. "Indian, my eye. Dead drunk, that's what he was. Falling down drunk." But Sally claimed she saw Jimmy Alseck pick up the blanket the next morning. Maybe it was Sarah Beth's Cherokee great-great-granddaddy. He's buried in that graveyard. Sarah Beth again. My secret twin. On my bad days I'd trade with her given some cosmic chance.)

***

Vaughn, Ken's disciple, was a year younger than us. He belonged to a fraternity but Ken persuaded him that fraternities were only for the bourgeois. Vaughn moved out of the frat house and Ken and he took an apartment together. Then they both dropped out of school. They had started their own secret society. One of Vaughn's former pledges, a sophomore, joined while staying in the fraternity. They called him their double agent, and he kept them up to date on whatever plans the fraternities had and then they worked at frustrating the fraternities, like throwing a stink bomb into the frat house one night when there was a dance. Pretty soon, though, Ken said that ruining the Greeks was kid stuff, and we went on to bigger things. In the meantime, James quit the society and two town guys who hung around campus joined up. And then there was me, the hillbilly, Ken's girl, and Jennifer, whose mother had raised her single-handedly and died of overwork and who grieved and who was nobody's girl. Jennifer was my only friend. (Nadira, my Pakistani savior, had gone home by then.) We confided all our woes and we discussed books and the ways of humankind. We helped Ken rob a liquor store to get funds for the shanty dwellers on the wrong side of town (we were ahead of our time), and when he used a little of the cash to buy some old dynamite, we wondered if that was the way to save humankind, but something had to be done, it was evident, and Ken's suffering face with its purple eyes and dark burst of beard persuaded us. Jennifer said it had to be at night when no one was there. But she was there, that woman, the newspapers said, doing some late-night catch-up work. We made the noise and the fire and we ran but not before I heard her scream. In my mind's eye only, after reading the next day's newspapers, I saw the blood and her arm lying separate. It still beckons to me in my dreams and follows my memory like the Indian after old man Simmons.

Ken and Vaughn went to prison not long after Jennifer did. They took all the blame and even tried to get Jennifer off the hook. There was nothing petty about Ken and his friends. Merely that they—we—confused our secret psychologies with the salvation of the world. Merely that.

Since the woman in the real estate office had lost only her arm, and since the damage done was less than it had sounded like, and since Ken's parents hired some high-powered lawyers, his sentence was relatively light. As the ringleader, he got ten years (but they let him out in five). I guess they figured that then they'd have to go light on Vaughn and Jennifer, too. They each served four years. I used to dream about Jennifer's incarceration at least once a week. She looked pasty-faced and cold as her fellow inmates swarmed over her like angry flies. I could never get past the bars to help her, and in my dream I knew that God, that old-fashioned Baptist God who's stern enough to frighten even the Baptist devil, was angry with me.

Did Ken go home to Scarsdale to the parents who sat every day in the courtroom and told the reporters their son was a good boy led astray? Did he become a surgeon or an accountant or a social worker like his ex-friend James? James went to see Ken in prison. Ken said he never wanted to hear from him again. What was he going through, then? Dejection? Depression? Or the idea of eluding the past altogether? In the short, infrequent letters James and I exchange, we never mention him or the reason why we have a short past in common. That's why the letters are so short.

I know what happened to Jennifer. She committed suicide the year after she left prison. I saw a photograph of her on the evening news, and I saw her dead body slumped across the grubby motel bed where she bought it. She took an overdose of something.

***

Orson looks beautifully old sitting up there on the platform. I don't really want him anymore. I like men who know a lot about books and Freudian psychology, ironic men. And what would Orson make of my secret life? Nonetheless, he is the only man who made me happy in that unreserved way that is supposed to attend true love. Perhaps it is not an ironic man I seek after all, but a post-ironic man. I fancy myself to be a post-ironic woman, after all.

> *"I will praise Thee, for I am fearfully*
> *and wonderfully made: marvelous*
> *are Thy works; and that my soul*
> *knoweth full well."*

One day in my adolescence as I wandered through the hills near my home, alone and dreaming, I came across a white shell with a blue interior lying among the leaves. Dreaming, I said, but often as I roamed it was worship. Every object—leaf, rock, bird, snake—harbored an intense life. My eyes were full of prayer. I heard a scholar say once that the earth is inscribable, that we plant not only seed there but also culture. And culture: how much of it is memory, that invisible architecture in which alone we feel at home?

Before entering church for the wedding, I climbed the slope to the minuscule Titwell cemetery, because I like to sit there among the peaceful dead and share with them the sunlit slope across the valley and the trickle of the little hollow that runs at the cemetery's side and the mysterious breath of the trees above the tombstones. Sometimes I caress my mother's headstone, for I loved her in spite of all and for good and sufficient reasons, the most important of which is that to the best of her ability she loved me. The few graves there are my passport to my life in Kentucky. My father, Arthur Titwell, and his brother came from North Carolina, leaving their family behind, bringing their class and their bought education like raiders into the beleaguered hills. Great-Grandfather Pelham, too, had come like a marauder, and his offspring lived frugal of children.

Afterward, I will sit down by the hollow and take my shoes off and let the clear water swirl about my feet, the incantatory bubbles. A mountain hollow falling through leaves on its way downhill inscribes my heart with passionate recognition. The thing itself. The thing in the air that never changes.

I wonder if my father is dead and, if so, where he is buried. His older brother, Charles, is buried here, along with his wife and firstborn, who died before I came into the world. I used to play with their other child, Sharon, when they came visiting from Louisville. She was pretty and, as she grew older, had the air of a phony Southern belle. How she cried at their funerals, though, clutching the hand of her tall, mild-looking husband. Luellen and I haven't seen them since. All our other cousins live in Virginia or North Carolina or farther afield. In this we are unnatural. Family is everything in Osier County.

Luellen is ten years older than I am. She married when she graduated from high school to a man who was loud and rough and sweet, and she tells me she never stopped loving him, though sometimes she wondered what it would be like to love someone else. She bore five children, who love her. Janice Sue, Matt, and Pettigrew (named after a Pelham, poor boy) live within easy visiting distance. Fred comes from Louisville with his family once a month or so. Ellen, in Indianapolis, makes it home two or three times a year. My sister has created the close-knit family we both yearned for when we were children. They came to visit me in Chicago once, Luellen and Tom and the five children. In the airport, I saw them before they saw me, my sister in a dated dress with her awkward husband firmly holding on to the luggage and the children compact around them. Light fell on her brown, frizzy mop of hair as she bent protectively over her young in vast, unknown O'Hare.

Luellen and I are very close now in some regards. In the days before Tom, her husband, was killed when a coal truck smashed into his car, in the days when their five children were young, when I was young, I would stay with the kids while Tom and Luellen had a rare date night. Once, James, my sweet ex, and I came down from Shaker Heights and, leaving the kids with Tom's mother (she's dead now), the four of us went square dancing in the old country music hall back of the courthouse. I was half in love with my own husband that night. Possibly, if we hadn't got married under such ridiculous circumstances, I would have loved him. When I called him back in March to congratulate him on his promotion, which had made the network news, he sounded content and confident. He seems really happy in his second marriage.

When I am here, Luellen and I sit around the kitchen table and gossip about our neighbors and the rest of the community and sometimes even mention world events. We watch over Janice Sue's children, and she lets me share their love without prejudice. She is not interested in my life beyond the hills but treats it like the playing field for some desultory game that I play when I am away from home. She knows nothing of Ken and the dynamite-shattered real estate office. She could not conceive that I would do such a thing. Or could she? I don't know. At this point I can't myself conceive of that unholy act, though it has defined my life.

Mother died several years ago. I was already living in Hyde Park. I had met Philip in my Chaucer class at the university. He was a Chicagoan, cynical and generous. When he got mad at me, he would mutter something about dumb Appalachians. I soon lost him, but then I hadn't invested much in him. At the time of Mother's death, though, it was spring break and Philip and I were planning a bus trip together to a cheap bed-and-breakfast in Wisconsin.

It was past midnight in my studio apartment with its rickety bed and the rusting kitchenette and the blue burlap curtains I'd made for the narrow windows. (And the roaches. No matter how often I bombed the place, there were some left, a soft-edged brown with ancient dirt from some unspeakable place.) The phone rang on the rickety little table beside the rickety bed. Philip was next to it, but he was not allowed to answer my phone. I leaned across his uncomfortable, half-sleeping bulk. Luellen said, "It's Mother, Darcy Anne." I knew right away that it was pretty bad.

"Is she in the hospital?"

"No, Darcy Anne. She's dead."

I heard Philip gasp as my elbow dug into his chest and I heard myself give out a long, deep wail.

So I went home for my mother's funeral. She'd had a heart attack while at the blackboard doing fractions for her fourth-grade students. Her granddaughter, Janice Sue, ran home, and Luellen called the doctor and then went back with Janice Sue. "She turned around," Janice Sue said. "Before she fell, she turned around and looked at me."

Years later I saw Robert de Niro do that, in the movie about a dying baseball player. He's behind the plate and then he's had it and he turns around slowly and looks at the strange new world. *Bang the Drums Slowly.* I thought immediately about my mother and the image and the sound—the song of the dying cowboy in Laredo—remain with me, but it's her form that I see spin slowly around to face the class that's half-afraid of her as they recede into some incalculable distance, some arithmetical equation with an Unknown. Perhaps death is like that, and we are estranged suddenly, not from ourselves, but from the world, which loses its immediacy, its meaning, its dimensions. We live by shadows, and what we do for each other is keep them at bay.

When I imagine the world as it will look in the moment before my death, I do not see cities or houses or even people;

I see green mountains overlapping beneath blue sky and the world is an enchanted wind sweeping the white clouds ominously, beautifully.

***

Besides Ken's "secret society" involved in our youthful crime, I have told only two individuals of my participation in it. One is James, and the other is Reena, a painter whom I met after I began teaching. She was giving lessons to a difficult, gifted student and we met to discuss the girl. We immediately hit it off in the way people sometimes do. Reena was homesick for Montana and disgusted with the 1970s political scene. She was down to earth and passionately idealistic at the same time. I would go to visit her and she would feed me bad wine and chicken curry made from scratch and show me her latest effort and curse the general inefficiency of the universe. Eventually, of course, we got to talking about ourselves, and Reena owned up to having been a juvenile delinquent, and we went from there until she got the whole story from me. The next year she went back to Montana to marry her high school boyfriend and when we met for a goodbye lunch she gave me a painting of two overlapping hills and a windy sky. I carry it with me everywhere, and even in Kentucky it harbors some secret about my distant childhood.

I was thinking of Reena last Wednesday when I left the store with a bag of banana flips. The grocery's porch looks out to Sarvis Mountain and an unnamed hill that is almost like its foothill. Mountains are never two-dimensional, and one's thoughts about them run concavely, convexly, shine and shadow. Back in the car, I took a drink from my thermos jug of coffee and then eased the old rattletrap out onto the dirt road that leads around back of Sarvis Mountain. It is a short road that once led to a house that is no longer there. Its owner went to Gary, Indiana, and got a job and came back and took his wife and children away, too. The place burned down one winter's night. Probably one of the overgrown young men who can't find work and don't for good or bad reasons want to leave built a fire to keep warm while he downed the last of his Southern Comfort. Or perhaps smoked his last joint. Or even snorted his last crack. (Somebody broke into old man Calhoun's place last week, beat him up, wrecked the place, and took the few dollars he had hoarded in an old cigar box.)

I went past the old Caskill graveyard, and then bigger timber at last, some of it ready for a second cutting, or was it a third or fourth? Luellen's old car jounced and spit up dust. Sun lay heavy on the windshield, supporting a hawk that circled about its invisible prey. Talking to myself about my late August return to Chicago, I turned off onto an old lumber road that reached deeply into the woods. Years had smoothed out its muddy ruts and seedlings grew from it here and there, scratching the bottom of the car. I went far in, into the dark woods, tall trees and underbrush hemming me in until I came to a large sun-dappled clearing. Entranced by the play of light and shadow, I stopped the car and got out before I saw the two men at the far side. They were passing something from hand to hand. I started to get back in the car, fast, when a once-familiar voice said, "Darcy Anne, it's just us." And it was just Orson and he was with Fergus. I started toward them, through the center. My feet disappeared in green stuff, and Fergus said, "Hey, woman, watch where yore steppin'." Though up to this I had seen those plants only in windowsill pots, I looked down and recognized marijuana weeds.

Orson asked, "Whatcha doin' out here all by yourself?" His words slurred a little and there was a small, loopy smile on his face that did not go with his smoothly combed silvery hair. This was as close as I had been to him in forty-five years, and he did not look well. His face had pasty patches, and faint dark rings threw into relief the bags under his eyes.

Fergus, on the other hand, looked very alert and feral. "I was hopin' I'd run into you one of these days," he said, looking at my breasts instead of my face. He was holding the joint that they had been passing back and forth.

In for a penny, in for a pound. "Where'd you get the makings?" I asked.

"Oh, I know me some good ole boys over in West Virginny," Fergus said. "Have my own pretty soon," he added, waving his hand.

Somewhere nearby, a redbird, a cardinal, said, "Purty, purty." It scared me that Fergus was actually telling me. I'd heard about his good old boys from Luellen. The word was that he got harder stuff than grass from them and was selling it to some of the miners at Flack Town and maybe even to some high school kids. There was an old shack over near Coon Creek that no (known) church members ever went near.

I was surprised at Orson. I knew that the two of them went way back. But Orson's essential decency was something I'd always been sure about. Not that smoking grass is indecent, but who you smoke it with can be. Aristotle in the deep woods.

"Whatcha you got there?" Fergus asked.

I realized I was carrying a bag full of banana flips and milk, enough banana flips to take some home to Luellen's grandchildren. "Banana flips and milk," I said defensively. It sounded comical even to my frightened ears.

Fergus laughed, but Orson said, "Hey, that sounds good. Can you spare any?"

Soon we were all three sitting on a thick cushion of moss, devouring little cakes, crumbs dropping around us, and Fergus was talking about the time he went to Chicago. "Stayed with my cousin Leroy," he said. "But I don't like the place. Too many people and too much noise. We had us a high old time, though," he said, looking at me speculatively. "How's about you, Darcy Anne? You like city life?"

I felt the moss dampness seeping into my skirt. "I guess I do," I said.

"You have you a high old time, Darcy?"

"Too busy," I said shortly and got up. "Well, I'd better be going. I forgot I promised Luellen I'd watch her grandkids this evening."

"It's a long time 'til evenin'," Fergus said, pulling at my skirt. "Sit back down, woman. We're just beginnin' to git reacquainted."

"Let go of my skirt, Fergus."

He tugged at it. "Well, sit back down, then." There was the anticipation of pleasurable trouble in his eyes.

Orson's hand shot out and clamped across Fergus's wrist. "Let 'er go, buddy."

"And what if I don't want to?"

"Just let her go."

Fergus looked at him and laughed but he let me go and I started toward the car.

"Wait," Orson said, "and I'll ride out with you."

The woods smelled old and full of damp dead leaves. I wanted rid of both of them, but Orson had possibly saved me from a bad thing.

"Oh, that's the way it is," Fergus said, but he was looking at Orson, not me, and he didn't seem to mind.

"No, that ain't the way it is," Orson said.

Fergus settled back against the thick gray bark of the tree and picked up the half-smoked joint. "See you later," he said, and I wasn't sure whether he was talking to Orson or to me.

Orson and I got in the car and I backed out until I found a wide place to turn around. "I'm surprised at you, Orson," I snapped, and my voice was trembling.

"Didn't you ever smoke a little grass?" he asked. "It ain't such bad stuff."

"I don't mean the grass," I said, and we rode in silence for a while, coming out onto the main dirt road. "Thanks, Orson.

I hope I didn't get you into trouble with Fergus."

"You didn't."

"But *why?*" I asked in a rising voice.

"Me and Fergus, you mean, I guess." He was silent and then said suddenly, "Let's go for a ride. Right on across the county line."

It had been a long time since I had had a one-on-one conversation with Orson. The feel of him sitting there next to me was at once alien and hauntingly familiar. "I don't play around with married men," I said without thinking.

"Lord, Darcy Anne, I never even thought about *that*," he said, shocked. "I just feel like gittin' out of here for a while. Course if you really gotta go tend Luellen's grandkids, that's different."

I felt on the threshold of something, but my upbringing reared its head, that and the fact that my sister Luellen was part of the community whether I was or not. "What if somebody sees us, though?"

"Not on this road, not this far out. We can cut across Painter Fork and when we come back you can put me down about here. I know a way home over the hill."

"Okay. Just show me how to cut across Painter Fork."

We went forward on that fine July day, Orson and I and the ghosts we brought with us. In a little while, I realized he was crying. "I'm dying, Darcy Anne," he said. "I'm dying."

I started to say the foolish kinds of things that people say, like "Are you sure?" and "Doctors can be wrong," but I didn't. "Does Sarah Beth know?" I asked.

"She knows and she don't know. She don't want to know."

"Poor Sarah Beth," I said.

"And me?" he cried out. "And me, Darcy Anne?"

"And you," I said, my own sudden tears making it hard to drive. I put my hand out to grasp his, and for a few minutes we went on like that.

He straightened up and pulled away his hand. "I'm sorry," he said, as though to a stranger.

"It's easier to tell a stranger," I said. I didn't know what to say next.

"How come you never got married?" he asked me.

"Well, I did, Orson."

"Oh, that's right. I remember somebody tellin' Sarah Beth. You met a boy up in Ohio. What happened to him?"

"We got divorced," I said. "A long time ago."

"No kids."

"No, no kids."

"He mean to you?"

"No. He was nicer than I was."

"Then how come you got divorced?"

"I didn't love him. He didn't love me."

"Why'd you git married then?"

"Maybe I'll tell you about it sometime." I could feel his curiosity subside into weariness. "You did all right," I told him. "Sarah Beth's a good woman."

"Couldn't have done better," he agreed.

"You still love her, then?"

"I do. I hate to leave her with nobody to take care of her."

"Sarah Beth'll know what to do," I said.

"Maybe that's what I'm scared of. My old woman up and marryin' somebody else."

Not without a decent period of mourning, I thought, not Sarah Beth. I didn't say it. "Well, you've been lucky," I said instead, "and I hear all your children turned out fine."

"I worry about Charlene. She don't seem to have her feet on the ground the way her ma does."

We were traveling up Painter Fork now. Arabesques of water in the rocky creek. An abandoned tipple.

"My brother Pete worked there for a while," Orson said. "It belonged to Wayne Cawry—you know, old George Cawry's son, the one that married Ronald Price's daughter."

I didn't know, not anymore, perhaps never did, so I just nodded.

"I'm sorry you lost the baby," he said suddenly.

"I was crazy about you," I told him. It seemed a small gift to give a dying man.

"You were a sweet girl," he said reminiscently. "But I was..."

"Crazy about Sarah Beth," I said wryly.

"You wouldn't have been happy," he said. "Look at you. Even been over to Europe, I heard."

"Well, so were you."

"Me? Oh, you mean the war. Well, that's different. Didn't see much of the place in one way and saw too much of it in another."

My wars were of another kind. "How long have you got, did the doctor say?" I asked him.

"Oh, he didn't come out plain, but I reckon about six months." We fell silent and then he said suddenly, "I saved Fergus's life once."

"He's bad, Orson."

"Not the part I know best," he said.

"I don't see how you can defend him."

"I don't. Don't defend myself either. Fergus is ever bad thing I never did. Never had to. He did them for me. If he's all bad, then maybe I am, too."

If some other woman had committed my crime for me, would I then be free of it—would I be good? Or would I be tied to her like a Siamese twin?

Orson and I spent the rest of that long afternoon on the road, across the county line, all the way to the Mountain Parkway, far beyond our inscribable past. We hardly talked. When I returned him across Painter Fork, he leaned across and hugged me before he got out and then went silently away. I felt it like a benediction.

***

Yes, that act of terror that I so will-lessly perpetrated in my youth has tyrannized my life. How clearly I see that as I move from the church house to the hall where the wedding feast is laid out, my eye on the landscape whose text is deeper in me than any other, deeper even than the short criminal text that has deformed me. I have lifted my eyes unto the hills, in that fine old text, and found a new strength. This evening I will tell my sister the truth, so that I might guiltlessly share her truth, too; and others, too, out there I will tell when intimacy or other urgency requires it, and I will move freely in the world again. Probably, in the technical sense, I'll get off scot-free. It was a long time ago, and I don't know any policemen. But if I don't, still I will be able to go to and fro among my presents and my pasts, among my loves.

Although she does not know it, Melissa Caskill has become my surrogate daughter. I cannot tell her how deeply pleased I am that she has chosen me to continue her past; that would be too much like favoritism. It continues my past also. I will do my best to shepherd her through her studies and to help her reach a tenable decision about where to spend her life. I myself have chosen a double life, acting every day in Chicago and other alien environs as though all my choices depended on this new past that I have created "outside." But perhaps I have begun to see my way clear to uniting my pasts. For don't mistake me, I love my life in Chicago. I am my mother's daughter and I find great satisfaction in being a teacher of the young, just as I find great satisfaction in the acquisition of knowledge. I love the city as well.

Standing here at the reception, partaking of Sarah Beth's homemade chicken and dumplings, I see Orson bending his head to hear something she is telling him and I find myself comparing him to Carl, the thin, ironic professor I met at the conference in D.C. the year before last. He was newly divorced and hurting; I was just lonely and hurting. We had a friendly lust for each other and a kind of academic camaraderie. Then he went back to Nebraska and I to Chicago. We get together once in a blue moon. It is to my credit, I suppose, that he is divorced. Once I did have an affair with a married man. To my credit there, he lied to me, telling me he and his wife were getting a divorce. They were not. I was young and, it is fair to say, dreadfully hurt when I discovered he went home to his wife most nights. I still saw him anyway because I was hooked, but I subsequently thought less of myself. In many ways I cling to the values of my childhood in such matters and, having dealt with this for decades now, no longer feel apologetic about it. And Orson is very much married to Sarah Beth.

But now, to my utter surprise, he comes over, towers above me, and asks in that husky voice that attends his illness if I am willing to "do some business" with him and will I meet him after the wedding at the old Alseck place right outside Sarvis, the small one where Orson is known to escape to after church, occasioning jokes among the Sarvis community. Sarah Beth's grandfather still owned it when I was a child, renting it out to one of the Lasco miners: the reason I remember being that as an eleven-year-old I had a crush on Jody, the miner's youngest son. He was in my class. My mother caught us kissing in the dark corner of the schoolhouse's rear wall. Hell to pay. For me. I imagine that Jody, to whose father Mother complained, got off easy. It was all a long time ago, like somebody else's fairy tale.

***

The path leading from Sarvis Road to the old cabin is no longer overgrown with horseweeds and rutted with many rains. Orson, who is waiting outside the cabin, tells me with some pride that he has spent the last two summers fixing the place up. "Come inside now," he says, somewhat awkwardly, "and see what I've done just since the warm weather hit." The cabin is still rustic enough, I think wryly to myself—no running water and no bathroom. He watches me look and says, "The well is up on the slope behind, Darcy Anne, and the outhouse is over to the right." He gauges rightly that I am still versed enough in country matters to want to know that the outhouse is far enough away from the well.

But I am looking at him now. He is still tall and lean, but he is woefully thin and his face has a dry look, and his eyes, those large hazel eyes that once gazed down into mine, are translucent. My eyes stray to his stomach, looking for a cancerous mass. "They cut it out, Darcy," he says gently. "Well, at least that part of it." I am indebted to this man for so many dreams, for my life's way. We look at each other and for a moment I feel that we might begin to redeem the past—my past, anyway—but even if I gave way to temptation, there would still be all my subsequent life and its turning—and, of course, there would still be Sarah Beth and their children and Sarvis and history.

"Want some coffee?" he asks, and I see that he has an old aluminum percolator.

"Of course," I say with something like real enthusiasm, and he actually grinds the beans and goes to the well for fresh water. We chat about our families until it is made, whereupon he pours some in a big green cup and passes it to me, shoving a bottle of cream—real cream, straight from somebody's cow—in my direction as I sit myself down in a cane-bottomed chair that somebody has recently re-caned.

"How's my granddaughter, how's Melissa doing up there in your neck of the woods?" he asks suddenly, and I feel a certain getting-down-to-business about the question.

"You've got a bright granddaughter on your hands," I reply truthfully, "and she seems to me to have a good outlook on life." I like my protégée.

"When she's talking to her grandmother, she mentions you a lot. And her and me have had a conversation or two about you," he says, half-teasing, but quickly adds, "Not that she knows anything. About you and me."

I look at his eyes, the flecks of gold among the brown, at

his lean, conscientiously shaven cheeks, their slanted brown planes, at his beautiful silver hair. At something like trust in those eyes. "There wasn't much to know," I reply, feeling an echo of that old loss but very much aware that it is an old loss and that, though I do feel attracted to him, I am aware that it is the attraction I might feel for any personable, intelligent man added on to the sweetness of our brief past. I might think, "if it weren't for Sarah Beth," but that isn't true. I am not the same person I was then. I have drawn a different map for myself. "What is it, Orson? What do you want from me?"

He is slow in replying. Finally: "You know us all so well, Darcy, and yet you are not one of us. One of us Caskills, I mean. And you've been looking from outside in on Kentucky, too, if you don't mind my saying that."

I do mind, but it is true.

"Melissa gave Sarah Beth that little book you wrote about Kentucky history, the one that Chicago company published, and I read it, and by God, Darcy Anne, it makes me want to become a Kentuckian. Which I already am." He reaches across the table and pats my hand in his enthusiasm and I feel it like a benediction.

"For someone to tell the truth about me and mine, Darcy Anne. I've got a hankering for that. I don't have the time left, and even if I did, I don't have the skill. I can't offer you money, at least not enough to make it worth your while..."

I interrupt, "I don't want your money, Orson, but I don't see that I am competent to tell that truth."

"Even if I tempt you with a piece of Kentucky? This piece? Come and look with me," he commands.

And I do. I take his hand and go to the door and see the blue-green pond, the old-fashioned rosebushes, the lilac bushes, and up on the slope of the mountain, the dogwood trees, and in my imagination the white sarvis blooms of early spring caught in the morning mist and the rose pink of the redbud trees. I see the dramatic curve of mountain against sky.

"I've kept it to myself," Orson half-whispers at my side. "No one ever comes here but me. I call it God's pond."

I see the landscape of my past captured, pinned down in my willing mind. Every summer and at other times I could come here and, like Orson, I could keep it to myself, a hidden treasure, a place where I could do Orson's work and my work. I see what I am being offered and what I must give in return. "Let me think about it, Orson," I say shakily. "I'll let you know soon."

And we leave it at that. I go away and he remains. As I leave, he tells me, "I spend Sunday afternoons here. My family understands that about me. Sarah Beth says it is my true church. She thinks I'm probably a heathen, and I am, I suspect."

The next day, when I go to the store to get my daily fix of banana flip, I run into Melissa. Usually when that happens, we say hello and isn't it a beautiful day and go about our different Sarvis lives, but today it is almost as though she's been waiting for me to come through the door, and while that can't be true, because I go at different times, it does seem that she has been metaphorically lying in wait for me. "Grandpa Orson says he had a conversation with you yesterday about writing about us and about...about leaving his Sunday pond to you." I begin to reply but she rushes on. "I just want you to know I think that's a good thing, Dr. Brant."

There is something argumentative in her declaration, as though she were traversing a dark passage with a feeble light. And surely this must be the case, else she would never have broached the subject here in her grandfather's store. Orson is not here today, but Melissa's father, Jeff, is behind the counter and isn't that Jolene, Sarah Beth's sister, over there in the post office section? As well as two customers, who are looking curiously at the two of us. I do a shushing look with my eyes and say, "I've got to rush, Melissa." I look at my watch. "Why don't you come by Luellen's in about an hour? Can you do that?"

She subsides, looks around, is relieved, but it is almost grudgingly that she replies, "Yes, of course. See you then."

I go out, bemused. I had not realized that Melissa was this close to Orson, that he would tell her what to me seems weighty family business before it was settled, before he told Sarah Beth and Jeff and Charlene. Or perhaps he has told them. Perhaps it is a family affair that has been hashed over and agreed upon. But why would they? I feel like a stranger who has butted in to something all too delicate. After all, that patch of land was in Sarah Beth's family for many years and perhaps they were counting on getting it back on the occasion of Orson's death. I am not good with these tangled family matters, having largely avoided them.

And here Orson is, inviting me into the thick of it, both in his request and in his offering. Panicked, I throw my banana flip and Coke into the car and hurry home to ask Luellen if it's all right if I take over the sun porch for a while, knowing that May Ellen and Joseph, my grandniece and nephew, are staying with their mother this weekend. Of course Luellen says yes, muttering that she will be in the garden anyhow. She mutters because, having some knowledge of her older sister's past, she isn't so sure about my associating with the Caskills—with Orson. I wonder, as I always do, if she has any inkling of my relationships with men. I wonder why we never discuss it. She would be willing to, I think, but I also think she would disapprove and be troubled. If I cling somewhat to my moral past, for Luellen its principles have never been past, but very much present.

When Melissa comes, her face is flushed with just-shed tears. I hurry her onto the sun porch, overlooking the cool, shaded, green creek and say to her before even the niceties of greeting have been observed, "It's all right, Melissa. I think myself that my writing a biography of your family would be an intrusive thing. And your grandmother must not like the idea of my taking over that pond?" I make the last statement a question. In fact, my whole reaction to Melissa's tears is a question. Partly a question to myself, because, looking at her lovely young face with Orson's hazel eyes ashine with Sarah Beth's steadfastness and moral fastidiousness, I find myself feeling maternal toward a young woman who is, after all, my dissertation student requiring respect and intellectual honesty. I say to myself, still panicky, that Orson's idea is ridiculous. What do I know about the Caskills, about the Alsecks, about their social and historical and personal histories?

"I'm not crying about Grandpa Orson's idea," she replies, looking directly at me in the way the young will, willing you to keep the trust they have been obliged to feel for you. "If you have been looking at my work, I have been looking at yours and there is a tender honesty in your approach that I appreciate."

I blush at the words "tender honesty." Only the young.

She continues without giving me room to turn away, metaphorically speaking. "It would be something, wouldn't it, to have someone with your track record keeping track of the Caskill family? Grandpa talked it over with me and Grandma before he approached you. He would never do something like this without talking to his Sarah Beth and of course it is from me that he has learned about you." She adds hastily, "Not that he didn't already know you in...ways I never will or could. Grandma Sarah Beth clued me in. Well, she was mainly guessing, but she guesses well and she loves him, you know."

So much for Orson's and my well-kept secret. Our melodramatic past brought down to earth and appraised by the next generation, to say nothing of Sarah Beth. Though I'm not so sure that Sarah Beth regards our mutual past with the dispassion she exhibits to her granddaughter. But then Sarah Beth is a lady, in the true sense of the word.

"You could help me," I say. "What if I gave you chapters to read and you got back to me on whether you think I'm on track?"

"I would like that," she says eagerly.

"I'll talk to Orson, then," I reply gingerly, "and probably I'll do it. But I want to think about the pond."

"He won't have you do the book if you don't accept the pond," she warns.

And with that we drop the subject and sit on Luellen's sun porch and discuss *The Tempest*, and I feel somewhat like Prospero in spite of myself.

After she leaves, I call Orson and Sarah Beth Caskill. Sarah Beth answers the phone and I hear her catch her breath after I say, "Sarah Beth, I've just been talking to your granddaughter and have decided to take on your and Orson's project."

"That's just fine, Darcy Anne," she tells me, and I hear that she has wholeheartedly decided to accept me in the role of family historian. "We'll have to get together. I have Orson's great-grandfather's diary and some other stuff you will want to look at." The way she gets to the historical nitty-gritty, I see that Sarah Beth obviously has more facets than I had been aware of. Well, after all, Melissa has told me that she and her grandmother are close. I feel a quick jealousy. "Hang on," Sarah Beth adds, "and I'll get Orson."

When his taut, husky voice answers, I jump right in. "I'll do it, Orson, but on one condition."

"What's that?"

"I know I'm going to spend most of my summers out by your pond, and I'm selfish enough to hang on to it until I die. But when I die, your pond goes to Melissa." So I lay my claim on Melissa, on the Caskill family.

He hesitates only briefly. "Why, that's right good of you, Darcy Anne."

"Maybe she won't want it?" I ask anxiously, because I know it matters. Because the whole thing matters, the Caskills and my Kentucky past—and future.

"Oh, but I happen to know she does," he says contentedly. "We just happened to talk about it the other day, but she felt I should offer it to you 'unconditionally,' as she said."

So, with Orson's—and Sarah Beth's and Melissa's—help, I have made myself an honorary Caskill. Orson is seeking to anchor his family and his home (Kentucky) securely in history, and I am honored and glad to be his anchor. Perhaps I will call my work "Sunday People," mostly ignoring Fergus and trying to keep its intentions on the level of the truer members of Sarah Beth's church, flawed and inconstant though they be.

It is true that you can't go home again, that you can't step into the same river twice, that you can't reenter your childhood. But it is also true that childhood doesn't have to become a fabled mythology toward which we yearn. It requires a lot of suffering, I think, before those of us who have been exiles can make of it rather the source of life that nature and culture have intended it to be, the place where all the threads of fate are anchored.

FERGUS

The minute I saw Luellen Titwell and that stuck-up sister of hers, I wished I hadn't come to this church today. Young Emile was a drinking buddy last summer but he won't have nothing to do with me now. Darcy Anne, that's Bertha's aunt's name. Fuck, I kissed her once. Wonder if she remembers. Cold little mouth. She wasn't cold with Orson that summer. One secret I got that I've kept for Orson. Sure as hell not for her. Thought I'd have a go at her, too, but she went away and didn't come back. 'Til now, and she's older, as old as I am, but I don't look it. She don't even sound like she belongs here. Wonder what and all she gets up to out there. Orson keeps *my* secrets. What he knows of them, which in one way is everything and in another way not fucking much. Ever since that day he found me where my uncle left me, hanging out to dry on a hickory tree.

> *"Hang your clothes on a hickory limb*
> *But don't go near the water."*

Used to sneak up by Orson's house and one of his sisters'd be singing that tune along with the radio. Little Drue—I

67

remember her long, fragile neck and those mournful gray eyes and her hands softly touching. I reckon my uncle meant to leave me up that tree until somebody took pity. Not him; he didn't take pity. How old was I? About seven, I reckon. Put a rope around my chest and hung me there. Orson told me to grab hold of the limb and he clumb up and cut the rope with his pocketknife. Crazy old man, Uncle Dennis. Finally drove off a cliff in that beat-up Chevy. Daddy cried. I guess I did, too, but I cried for my pa, not for no Uncle Dennis.

Orson and me played together back up in these hills and waters, and I was the one who taught him how to catch catfish with his hands, sneak up behind one and grab it back of its gills. Daddy taught me. When Daddy died in that rockfall in the No. 4 mine, Orson cried for me, but I didn't cry, not for Daddy, not for me. By then I'd learned cryin' don't do no good. Better to make other people cry, the way I did Uncle Dennis's son, my cousin Joshua. It was after Daddy died, though, that I done that to Joshua. The red truck had come and got Ma, like we used to say, and she was in the crazy place up in Lexington. We'd been living way up at the head of Shady Hollow after Daddy died, livin' on peart nigh nothing. Old Mrs. Byrne down the holler gave us vegetables, and Aunt Clara Jean and Uncle Rob gave us some canned pork, but it warn't enough. We drunk a lot of water, I remember that.

Before they strip-mined back up in that holler, water on Juniper Mountain would pool up beneath some sticks that acted like a dam and Orson and I would cup our hands. In winter there was ice in it: cold as God's breath against my red, cracked hands. Even Orson had disappeared, back into Sarvis Mountain, into the warm house up on the flat.

I was there by myself after they took Mommy, and Joshua came up the holler and said he was my boss now and I'd better do like he said. Took the last bite of food in the house and held his gun on me and told me to take off my shoes and wade in the holler. It had a thin skim of ice on it. I did like he said, all right, and he thought he had me ready to shit my britches. He looked away, and I picked up that big wet rock and threw it. Always had a good aim. Knocked him out cold. I drug him over to the holler and pulled his shoes off and put his feet in and left him there. He lost three toes, by God. Swore he'd get me, but he never did. I had a gun, too, and I could use it better'n he could. Orson said he was crazy. "No matter what you want to call it," I said, "he's mean. But I'm meaner." The minute I put Joshua's feet in that ice water, I felt some part of me go winging off like a bird and I was free. Maybe it was my soul. Well, I finally took care of Joshua. Held my own in the pen. Had 'em eating out of my hand.

But that was all right because Orson and me didn't believe in all that religious stuff. Orson shrugged his shoulders and said it made life easier for some. But I thought only for weak people. Better to see clear, then you could see what was comin'. We hid behind the elder bushes that Sunday and watched Preacher Ames baptize Orson's Aunt Abby, her hollering and screamin'. Orson made a sound like that old black painter that had a home somewhere back up Shady Holler. A painter's got a cry like the devil's ghost, and them Baptists didn't know whether to go or to stay. The preacher took Orson's aunt down while them on the bank shifted from one foot to the other and the women started gatherin' the young'uns up. Orson let out another cry and the preacher let go and Orson's aunt fell backerd in the creek. I almost choked tryin' to keep from laughing. But old man Peters run over to his car and got his shotgun so Orson and me hightailed it outta there.

Orson's family don't want no part of me: Sarah Beth never liked me, 'specially not after I felt Charlene up a little. Well, I wish I hadn't done that. I was high on the weed, I reckon. Sarah Beth didn't like me anyhow, but before that business with Charlene she was scared she was goin' to. Because of that kiss, I reckon. Silly bitch. It didn't have nothin' to do with her. And me touchin' Charlene didn't have nothing to do with *her* neither. I was tryin' to get rid of Orson while I still could. He's the weight that brings me down to earth (like he did when he cut me down from the tree). If Orson had come after me, I reckon I'd've killed him. Then I would have been as free as Judas.

What Orson thinks about that time in the woods? He laid an arm around my shoulder to comfort me after Daddy died and then it turned into somethin' else for me and he knew it. Turned away. We never talked about it. Orson sittin' up there on the platform, his eyes caressing those two youngsters getting married. He knows I sell the weed but he don't know about the crack. He just as much as told me he'd turn me in if I sold hard stuff. Doing it behind Orson's back. But if he found out? I won't go back to the pen.

I went over to West Virginny, to Logan County, when I was twenty and didn't know no better. Got me a job in a mine where you had to crawl through the puddles. And a damp wind blowing. My buddy was missing two fingers on his right hand. Funny, smooth, round nubs where the knuckles should've been. Second day, I slipped in some grease and almost broke my neck. My buddy told me the company didn't use enough roof support. Not that he was my real buddy. We helped each other out on the job, like mine buddies do. Crawlin' along up toward the face with a crick in my neck and my back expectin' the whole shebang to come tumblin' down on me. My lamp shining in the puddles making pictures of hell. It was that poker game on Saturday nights that saved me, and that lean, mean Charley sellin' us them sweet-smellin' hand-rolled cigarettes. I plumb took to grass, but I didn't let it get hold of me. Got friendly with Charley, and we figured out how I'd be his salesman across the state line and I went home to Kaintuck.

Not before I killed me a rattlesnake, though. He was the foreman on my section. We had a run-in right off because I don't kowtow to any man, and he kept me workin' at the face all the time, on the miner machine, them big old jaws biting the coal and chewing it and spitting it out into the shuttle car. The noise peart nigh drove me crazy. I swallowed enough coal dust that if you threw a match in I'd probably glow. Better that than a roof bolter, goin' where they blow everything up and then stick in a few timbers. I seed this feller go in and I heard a big noise and nobody come out. The roof fell in. I don't reckon they ever did get his body. That foreman rode me goin' in and he rode me comin' out, 'cause I was young and 'cause I sassed him back, no other reason. I can't remember his name. Caught him comin' out after dark and follered him up the hill. We fought and I picked up a rock and smashed his pumpkin head in. First time I killed a man. There he was and then there he wasn't.

Orson sitting up there on the platform looking over at his lady. That Sarah Beth of his, she'd be a Naomi, I reckon. Orson's cheeks all hollow. Won't be long now. I said, "You aimin' to make peace with God or just to get Sarah Beth off your back?" I thought he'd say somethin' like "Little bit of both, Fergus, little bit of both," and give that grin of his. But, no, he said, "Wouldn't hurt you none to come to church once in a while, Fergus. Wouldn't hurt you none at all." And here I am. But mainly I'm here for Orson. Not for God. If God is, he declared war on me a long time ago and I declared it right back. Lucifer. "Bright of visage, dark of deed" in that book on the library table in the schoolhouse. Miz Titwell made me sit in the back row, and she switched me that time I was fighting with Emory Jones. She didn't switch me agin. I caught up with her that day after school and said, "You switch me agin I'll hit Luellen in the head with a rock." She thought I meant it. One day she caught me reading at the library table and shook her head and said, "It's a pity you'll never amount to anything, Fergus." I knowed what she meant, too. I kept my pride instead. I liked sitting in the schoolroom in the spring when the insects were hollerin' outside and the birds were fussing in the trees and I knowed I'd be getting' out soon and maybe

71

I wouldn't even bother to come back. But I made it through the eighth grade. Even went to high school for a couple of days. They threw me out when I beat up Tommy Lee. He had it comin' to him. Talkin' about my ma being in Lexington.

There Ma sits, not ten feet from Darcy Anne Titwell, all crippled up now with arthritis. I saw she was goin' to church every Sunday and I asked her why she didn't join. "The day you're ready to join, I will," she said. She chooses me over her god. I don't believe nothing I can do would free me of her. If I put my hands around her throat she'd bless me while she choked. Maybe she is crazy.

Ma's people go way back, at least as far as the Civil War. We ain't got ours showing like Sarah Beth's colonel in a far courtyard or her grandparents' pictures up in church. Ours is in a little oak trunk given my ma by her daddy, and he told her the trunk was made special for what it held of his grand-pappy. There's a Union Army uniform in there fallin' to pieces. And there's a letter my great-great-grandpappy got from his brother. He owned a restaurant in London, England, and he must've made good money at it because he was offering to pay for Great-Great-Grandpappy to come back home. "Father forgives you," it says. I wonder what Great-Great-Grandpappy did. Anyhow, he didn't go home but left Pennsylvania and come on down the Ohio River and then headed south. I'm glad Ma thought to bring the trunk along when we got kicked out of the coal camp. They's a part of me locked up in that old thing, and someday I'm going to let me out and see if I can stand it. Crazy talk. I'm Ma's son, all right. And Uncle Dennis's nephew, I guess.

That's what she used to say, the tears wetting her face and dripping from her like rain from a tree. "There's a part of me locked up in that old trunk." Then she'd laugh. "Someday I'll jump out and say 'BOO.'"

But none of *my* secrets are in the trunk. I didn't catch the blood of my cousin Joshua when I finally killed him. I didn't catch Minnie's screams after I choked her newborn.

It was a pore thing, anyhow, and it was mine as much as hers. He put his little fingers around my one finger and I knew it was him or me. Done him a favor, I reckon. But Minnie got up and walked out. She turned around at the door and said, "The only way you can stop me goin' is to kill me, too," and she meant it. I let her go. Buried the baby. I heard she let out it died of croup.

The thing is, I don't feel sorry. The day I feel sorry I'll either kill myself or join the church or maybe both. Because it's in me somewhere, at the edge of dreams like a rat gnawing a little here and a little there.

Daddy taking me to town to see the circus. It come up all the way from Florida, he said. We took the train in. When I was little, the train still run through here, stopped at Sarvis Junction on its way to town. "I ain't never seed a circus myself," he said. "Your Ma's helpin' your Aunt Clarrie out. Let's me and you go see us a circus." I must have been knee-high to a grasshopper then and I didn't want to be free. I put my hand in his big old miner's hand with the black under his fingernails and one nail growed black and thick and the joints too big, and we went off to the circus. I was right taken with the yellow wagons and their red trim but the clowns scared the shit out of me. They made me laugh when I didn't want to laugh. They looked like a fever that I was going to catch. And I knew right off about the animals. They didn't like being cooped up and caged up. I figured they'd kill somebody give 'em half a chance and I didn't blame them. Daddy liked the clowns but he felt that way about the animals, too. People say he was a no-good, unfeelin' bootlegger but he only helped out Uncle Robbie a little.

Yes, my daddy was a good man. Wonder how he had a son like me? Killed off, killed dead in that rock fall, smashing his head like a pumpkin. Maybe I went crazy, too. Orson'd say that ain't no excuse, but only if I asked him. He don't volunteer. I bet you they ain't a thing Orson ever done his pa wouldn't look down from heaven and say that's all right. Well, except for an extra woman or two.

I swear them preachers in this place think in pairs. Once, when I came, it was Naomi and Ruth, then it was Abel and Cain. *"The voice of thy brother's blood crieth unto me from the ground, and now art thou cursed from the earth."* But why did God turn down Cain's offering and take prissy-mouthed Abel's? God should have been Abel's keeper, since he liked him so much.

"Two coats lay before me
An old and the new
And I could have either
And what must I do?"

I hate it when they sing, long ups and heavy downs like God himself must've died in the night. Orson's put on his fine new coat now, but I'll stick to the earthly coat, by God, and it won't be ragged neither. Mornings while the coffee makes, I hum this one song Daddy liked. Mostly he liked songs with women in them, like "Pretty Polly, Pretty Polly," but he used to sing:

"O come angel band
Come and around me stand.
O bear me away on your snowy wings
to my immortal home.
O bear me away on your snowy wings
to my immortal home."

Giant white butterflies flocking through the woods. When I was little, I could see them.

Daddy and me wadin' through the creek fishin' on a hot summer day, sun melting on our heads and our legs cold in the water. "There's a big 'un down there by that old log, Fergus, throw your line real quiet." We'd go home but she was never there, over at Aunt Clarrie's maybe, helpin' put up peaches. She hated the coal camp and that slag mountain by the railroad and the trash over the riverbank and coal dust on everything. Or she was back in the woods up Shady Hollow talkin' to herself. I give that to them Lexington people; she don't hold long conversations with herself no more and she don't cry all the time. I'm not in her oak trunk, maybe.

Drusilla. Maybe I'm in the grave with Drusilla. No, her god wouldn't let me in there. I'm an angry ghost hovering above her tombstone, waiting for a crack to appear so I can go down into that dark hole and keep her company. That one time we met upon Indian Rock. The only time she agreed to meet me somewhere. She come out of the woods onto the rock and looked down at me making my way up. The sun was shining on her hair so it looked like a dark shadow above her face, her eyes in shadow too, looking down at me and thinking what I don't know. When I got up there I saw she brung a basket of food. I couldn't eat for the want of her. She listened to all my talk of the things Daddy had taught me about the woods. Where the most walnut trees were. How to soften willow bark in the creek. How to hunt a wild pig. I used to know all these things I don't know anymore because I am filled up with my life. I reached out at last and held her hand and she let it rest there for a moment and I felt the promise of salvation. The next week she was dead. I thought it would kill me. I was almost dead of anger that night. *God taketh away*, they say. Well, goddamn God. I was free to go my own way now, except for Orson, but he's more like a looker-on in my life now where Drue sat in the middle of it and left the dark hole into which I pour my spite. And except for Ma. If anybody told her about the things I do, I'd kill them.

When Orson told me that the doctor said there wasn't nothing more he could do for Orson, he said it like it was happening to somebody else. I always admired that Orson could do that. I got in my pickup and drove all day and all night and part of the next day. It was April and nature changed from green to snow as I drove north, keeping myself going with coffee so hot it burned my throat. Could have sued if I was the suing kind. I got other ways of settling my scores.

In midafternoon, I pulled into this little town, half froze to death because I didn't have a coat on. I had plenty of money, though, and some weed, most of which I sold for the hell of it to two boys who came swaggering out of the high school in imitation leather jackets. Then I swung into Sears and bought me a coat and gloves and heavy socks and some new jeans and a plaid flannel shirt. I asked the man who waited on me if there was any place to stay nearby and he told me to go north out of town until I got to the North Trail Motel. Once I was out of town, I stopped by the creek and made mud and smeared it on my license plate.

The motel could've used a coat of paint to cover the rust and the water stains. There was a drunk man coming out one door with a phony blonde. What I call a quickie motel. They ain't no different wherever you go. The only thing I got against my life is the kind of company I keep.

I gave a phony name and got my card and went to the room to take a shower and change. The dirty shades were drawn and the room was like a Frigidaire. I made myself look good and went down the concrete steps and over to the bar and restaurant, where I ordered a hamburger and beer and started looking around. It looked so flat it scared me. Flat and distant. These people didn't know about me and they didn't care one way or the other. They didn't care much about themselves either.

After I finished eating, I took my beer and went over to the table where three men were drinking whisky and telling each other dirty stories. I introduced myself (with my phony name) and said I was a stranger in town. One of them, a bald-headed feller in a cheap suit, invited me to join them. We told some more dirty jokes. When they were drunk enough, I invited them back to my room to play poker. "I'll take you up on that," said the skinny guy with the red nose. I could tell he thought he was pretty good.

So the supermarket butcher (the bald-headed guy), the insurance feller (the skinny one), and the jailhouse janitor (he was dark-complected and a good dresser) came back with me to that dirty little room. But first I got the deck of cards I always carry in my glove compartment, and the skinny one went across to the liquor store and got a bottle of whisky. Then we settled down. I let them win some so they wouldn't leave. The bald-headed guy had a wife and four kids on the other side of town. The skinny one was about to get married for the second time. The janitor liked to chase skirts, he said. What about me, they asked, and I told them about my sweet little wife down home in Virginia.

Oh, we were buddy-buddy. I looked at the clock and saw it was past midnight and I needed to be far down the road before daylight. I went to the closet and got out my gun, the silencer on and ready for use, and shot them dead. Bham, bang, bham. In the head. I took all their money just for the hell of it, wiped all the surfaces I'd touched. I'd made sure there wasn't that many. I hightailed it out of there. When I let myself out, there was a light, cold rain that felt like milk on my face. That was half a year ago. Never learned what happened afterward, who they thought they were looking for. Like it never happened. I wanted to tell Orson about it, say I did that because of you. He'd turn me in.

He's gone over to God's side. Sitting up there looking across at Sarah Beth. I always thought someday he'd bust out. Guess I was wrong. Might as well be. He's my brother anyway. What will happen to me when he is gone? I've done everything to be free of him. There'll be nothing left to hold me then. I'm played out, done with it all. Lost. Sarah Beth has won.

SARAH BETH

How many Sundays have I gone up this road? When I began, it was a dirt road and I was a baby in my mother's arms beside Daddy, who held the reins as our two plow horses pulled the unpainted wagon. When Orson and I were courting, they laid gravel on the road, and he came by for me in that old beat-up Model T. When Charlene was ten, they blacktopped the road and I sat beside Orson in our old blue DeSoto. He called that car Huldie and I used to tell him he treated it better than he did me. The children in the back seat, all three of them by then. When Charlene was fifteen, the members got enough money together to build the new brick church. I always preferred the wooden one that Granddaddy and the members built with their own hands. Plain and white sitting among the trees below the graveyard. Now we just use it for dinners and meetings—and wedding receptions. I'm not real happy about Emile marrying Bertha Titwell. The Titwells have always been so stuck-up, even Luellen, though she's friendly enough. But Emile and Bertha look beautiful together and look at the way she's beaming at him.

Orson is dying. What can I do? What will I do?

Roger Alseck's old Chevy was just in front when we came up the hill. I saw that dent where his son backed the truck up against it last fall. My third cousin, or is it fourth? Let me see now. Roger is Great-Granddaddy's brother Packard's grandson. Packard's son Chiltern married Janie—no, it was her sister. Tabitha Jones. Roger was their last child. He was born on my first birthday. Getting up there in years. Like me. Like Orson.

A row of dusty cars up the summer hill, eating Roger Alseck's dirt. Mommy named her oldest son Roger too, but he died of croup. That little grave to the left as we go up on the graveyard. I still make flowers for the graves for Decoration Day. When I was a child, we would go to Orson's daddy's store and get the packets of crepe paper—blue, red, yellow, green, pink, whatever Mr. Caskill carried. Making the flowers out on the back porch with my daughter Charlene, and before her with Mommy. Mommy's white fingers wielding the scissors, curving the squares into rose petals, winding green around the wire stems. Now I do that part. Daddy never wanted Mommy to work in the garden. He bragged about her white skin.

There's really not enough room by the church for parking. I remember ten or twelve years ago, Mary Ellen Newell wasn't thinking and pushed on the gas instead of the brake. She's lucky she come out of it with just a broken arm and a sore stomach. She'd have gone all the way down to the creek if that oak tree hadn't stopped her.

This hard bench feels resentful beneath my thighs. Anderson Rathbone and his Victoria sitting in the back. My sister Jolene and her husband Burt whispering to them. Jolene told me Anderson's been stepping out on Victoria, with some woman on the other side of Osierville. Don't see why. Victoria's a pretty woman, and a good church member, too. But knowing Anderson, that's the problem. She's too good for the likes of him. Wonder what he's been doing Saturday nights now that they tore down the old train depot (I'll ask Orson). Miners taking their pay there and playing poker, coming home with nothing. Jolene's Burt used to be real bad for coming home with his pay gone and the grocery bill due. Mommy didn't want her to marry Burt. "Look at his family," she said to Jolene. "Shiftless and ornery." Mommy didn't usually say things like that. She was a lady. But Burt's been a good man. Good to the children. Good to Jolene. He quit gambling after Jolene threatened to take the children and leave him. Orson gambled too until I took a cue from my sister.

Jolene and Elswick and me. Three of us, like my own children. Jolene says I'm like Mommy. Jolene likes to use a curse word now and then, and she says, "I'm not a lady like you, Sarah Beth." We love each other, my sister and me, but we don't like each other too much. She always used to fight with Daddy, and when he died she sort of shrugged and turned away. Daddy's body lying in the open casket. Flowers smelled too sweet. I looked in and it wasn't him. A thing lying there. I feel him there when we go to the graveyard, him and Mommy both on the green hill, the blue sky singing.

After Daddy died, we sold the home place to Taggart, the lawyer from town. That gave us Charlene's college money. They tore down our old home (the room where we were all born, the blue wallpaper with its white blooms), and Orson helped build Taggart's big brick house on the hill where the rhododendrons used to bloom. The home place was down in the big field. My bedroom on the second floor looking over the garden out back. Row of hollyhocks at garden's edge. It was Great-Granddaddy's house, with the slate roof he put on by himself. Coming back to it after church, the broomsage hill and then the cornfield on one side and the tobacco patch on the other. Beehives in the side yard, and the smokehouse. Hickory smoke. Never have hams that good anymore. Mommy's washing place out back. The smell of ashes. Her lye soap, too strong to use all the time. She wouldn't let me help stir it in the tub.

Cousin Cora, who long ago left for Indiana with her husband, would come over and help on wash day. The time she and I ate the brains right out of the hog's head after it roasted in the oven. I told my granddaughter about that the other day, and she put her hands over her ears. But frog legs, that's all right because she hears they eat them in Paris, France. I still fry the chicken head when I kill a chicken. The brains. My favorite piece. Melissa won't look at me when I'm eating it.

Melissa loves her grandpa. Dip of snow-white hair across his brow. A bird's wing. Orson.

I see Darcy Anne Titwell sitting in the front row down below, smiling across at Melissa. Melissa likes her, likes working with her on that paper she's writing. Me a young bride and Darcy stopping us and putting her hand on Orson's other arm and lingering it there while she said hello. Not to both of us. Just to him. Here was this stranger, I don't think I'd ever said more than two words to her except in passing, laying some kind of claim on my new husband. She walked away then and I looked over at Orson. Stranger. Who was he that Darcy Anne Titwell put her hand on his arm? She was the teacher's daughter, the banker's daughter, and she was going to college up in Ohio.

Time for the reception, over in the old church, where I feel I belong. Anderson and Victoria pass me on my way to link hands with Orson and Victoria says hello. "You're lookin' fine, Sarah Beth," she says in her pretty soft voice. "How's Orson doin'?" She doesn't look so good herself. Probably catching on to Anderson's two-timing ways.

"Fine, honey. Did your Aunt Georgia come last Saturday?"

"All the way from Lexington. Fenton didn't come, though. He went fishing over in Menifee, down by Cave Run."

"Orson and Jeff are talking about doing that next weekend."

"Is Orson up to it?"

I throw up my hands. "Did you ever try to keep a man from doing something he's got his heart set on?"

Woman talk. The boys on one side of the schoolyard and

the girls on the other when I was young. But not my deepest thoughts. Nobody to hear them but God. We talk about life and death and who's coming to supper and who's sick and who's two-timing who, but we don't talk our private thoughts. Between me and God out in the garden. Does he hear me? On a regular Sunday we go back and forth, up and down the aisles, shaking hands and saying hello and God bless you and how's Uncle Solly?

Brother Lyman is shaking hands with Orson. Tilde Lyman's son. I remember when him and Elswick got falling-down drunk. They wrecked Lyman's old Ford and Lyman fell out of the car on top of Elswick. "Don't die on me," Elswick is supposed to have said. "Don't die on me." Well, they both lived, the rascals, and now Lyman's a preacher.

And my brother Elswick's in Detroit. The first year he went up there, he came home one weekend, shaking his head, but he didn't say why. For years he was tired and pale. Then he married Gina. She's got a mouth like a truck driver, as Orson says, but she's good-hearted enough. Wonder what her people are like. Italians. Elswick rubbed his big belly and smacked her backside. "All that spaghetti," he said. She sat down on his lap and bit his ear. I turned my head away. In front of the children. Orson laughing with them, looking at her red lips and black hair. Men. After they left, he shook his head and said, "Fool woman. She must use up a lipstick a day." That was to make me feel better. He sent Jeff and Charlene out to play and said, "Come and sit on my lap, woman." And I did. Probably when Tessie was started. Long ago.

Harlen Jones pulls Orson aside. His wife just dead, poor man. They say the doctor was treating her for sugar diabetes when she didn't have it. The insulin killed her. Orson's brother went into that hospital just to have his appendix out and they left something in there. Nearly killed him. And Virgil Pauley's Suzie, she's had thirteen operations. Couldn't have needed all of them, could she? Seems like everybody's dying of cancer. From the mining maybe. They're cutting the top off Rendell Mountain now. Mammon. What if they took off Sarvis Mountain?

Great-Granddaddy and -Grandma look biblical in their photographs up there on the wall. That old black suit and his beard down to here, white and curly as the prophet's. And she has on a black dress and that high collar, her hair in a bun just like mine. Long, long hair. When Orson first took mine down, he wrapped it around my waist. I can't help but feel proud that my great-grandparents started this church. Nothing but wooden benches under the trees at first, and then everybody got together and built the old church, not the one we call old now but the one before it, the one that burned down in the Civil War, leaving the big old hickory tree out in the side yard by the creek. Daddy always said them nuts tasted better than any other hickory nuts. He'd pick up a bag of them in the fall and save them for Christmas eating and cookie-baking.

God be praised, Daddy would say. When he preached, he never went in much for the hellfire, and Grandpa would shake his head from side to side and tell him he was too weak. But Daddy thought God had a sense of humor. Wonder they didn't throw him out. They did throw out Uncle Benjamin, who thought Jesus was just a spirit. Poor Uncle Ben, up there in that asylum in Lexington. Grandpa sitting out there at the edge of the yard watching the sunset, silent. "Don't bother him, girls," Mommy would say. She treated her daddy like he was the right hand of God. Uncle Benjamin went right out of his mind after they threw him out of church and wouldn't let him preach.

I remember the time Orson and I went to Lexington. Our honeymoon. How can I forget it when Orson brings it up so much? He's real proud of that trip, proud of me, he says, though Lord knows why. We did stop at the asylum and spent an hour with Uncle Benjamin, who hardly said a word the whole time we were there. Unhappy people saying strange things and making strange moments. It was cold in there, too. That was the first time I'd been in a big city, if you don't count the time I went to the hospital with Mommy when Daddy was dying. It got to be ordinary for me later on, when Charlene was at UK and we'd go up and visit her. And then when Orson had to go into the VA hospital, I stayed with Charlene and Bob. I hated that. The trouble between them shouting out for attention. Sitting long hours, long nights with Orson. And then going back for the chemo. Orson sick as a dog. Twice, he went through that. The third time he refused to go. I begged him to, but he said, "They done pretty much told me my days are numbered. Why would I want to go to Lexington and maybe die away from home, Sarah Beth?"

When Daddy was dying, Mommy cried every day and for the first time *I* had to comfort *her*. We stayed at that place near the hospital, Mommy fretting over the money every day. We only stayed three days. The noise, and it was on a street where the houses looked dirty and the grass was brown. (Not like Charlene's pretty house. She said it was Federal: brick with white trim.) Thank the Lord they released Daddy then. Home to die.

But when Orson and I went for our honeymoon—except for our visit with Uncle Benjamin—we just saw the rows of brick houses and pretty yards and then stores with pretty clothes and jewels in the windows. People looked at us like we weren't there, hurrying on by. I could see we were dressed wrong. In the hotel, too, up off the ground, people walking by without looking. Orson soon got the hang of it, but I didn't. Nobody I knew. I couldn't have proved that I was Sarah Beth Wright Alseck Caskill if I'd had to. Didn't even have a driver's license back then.

That evening, Orson went to meet his Army buddy. He said he wouldn't be gone long. His buddy wasn't married, so he didn't take me along. Said they were going to have a beer in a place where women weren't welcome. I went down to the hotel restaurant for supper, feeling like a drawing on the blackboard, half of me erased. I wasn't dressed like the other women, and I didn't talk like anybody but the waiter and he was too busy to talk. Maybe that's why Charlene went the other way and took up with town folks. Home. The damp cold feel of spring dirt on my feet. The green scratchy feel of beans growing. The whippoorwill back in the woods when it's getting dark. The silence.

But now we have the television. Silence gone, and you can't talk back to TV people. They have it all their own way, and the kids pick up Lord knows what. Feel 'em up. Shoot 'em up.

Orson has his rifle. Him and Jeff go up to Menifee County to deer hunt. Drunks out there waving their guns around. Someday one of mine'll get shot. A rifle is a beautiful thing when it gets shined up. Made to do something and does it well. I like that, but I hate what it does. Orson's war souvenir, that German Luger, is an ugly thing.

My great-great-granddaddy, the Cherokee, got shot with a rifle and him unarmed, the story goes. (Orson has always been crazy about the fact that I really am part Indian.) I can see my Cherokee ancestor now, coming across the ridges, all the way up from North Carolina. His hair in a braid, was it? and sloe eyes above arching cheekbones. Coming across the ridge, tall and thin and muscles in his arms, his skin shining in the noonday sun, thinking Lord knows what. I wish I knew. Next time Jeff and Bernice bring Melissa with them, I'll ask Melissa to order me a book on the Cherokees off the Internet. Now why didn't I think of that before?

Coming across the ridge to home five years later and, boom, that soldier shoots him. Some ragtag kin of the Puseys got up to be a Johnny Reb. Reckon he thought a redskin was fair game. Or did he know something we don't know? Was my Cherokee ancestor a Union man? Good thing he only shot him in the leg. And Great-Great-Great-Granddaddy took him home. What did my great-great-grandmother think when she first saw her future husband? Did she herself look like Ma? Like me?

I should be thinking about Orson. I quickly glance sideways at him and his hand tightens on mine. My husband, my beau. He's good-looking yet, that wave of hair dipping down on his forehead. Just like when I first noticed him, before he went off to Italy, to the Big War, except that his hair is white, white.

My kin Roger Albany Alseck was a Union soldier for sure. But he slipped over and warned his cousin who was a Confederate spy that the Union captain was coming with his men to capture him. They both lie up there in the graveyard, along with Colonel Alseck. I can't help feeling proud to have a Revolutionary War colonel in the family. God forgive me if it's a sin. That statue of him in Belle Market right in front of the courthouse. Orson always joking about marrying up in the world.

Orson lying in that hospital bed and not knowing who I was, oxygen mask half hiding his face.

What he has stood. Lying in that hospital in Italy, all his buddies dead or moved on or in some other hospital. Only lately he's talked about the war. Not like Orson to let on he's afraid of anything. (He'd just crack a joke.) Clutching at me in his sleep. Just a boy then, never away from his family before. Never out of the hills. And then, bang, bang. Buckets of sun in Italy, he said, splashed all over the place. And Italian girls, oh la la la. But he still doesn't talk about the shooting part of it. Wonder if he got to know any Italian girls. That way. He wouldn't tell me.

I see Brother Johnson going into the old church door. Last time I heard him preach, he said at the beginning he was going to prove beyond a shadow of doubt that being saved brings us grace in this world too. Then he talked about Joseph and how he was saved from the pit and from Potiphar. I liked it when he talked about Joseph's daddy and then about his own daddy, about how they were real poor one winter and how his daddy went into debt and got him a warm winter coat and cap and put them under the Christmas tree.

The time is swiftly rolling on,
When I must faint and die,
My body to the dust return,
And there forgotten lie.

I had just got married when Mommy died. Couldn't have been over three months pregnant. She wanted to live until I had that child. We did not bury her in the Wright graveyard but in the Alsecks', not in her family's but in Daddy's family's. Even in death women go where their men go. We are wanderers who lose our homes. Just looking for a home. We make homes. Wherever they take us. Orson stayed right here and he never minded when my kin came to visit, and he says he wants to be buried here, not on the other side of Sarvis Mountain where his pa and ma are buried and poor Drusilla. My granddaughter Melissa, who calls herself a "feminist," says that's great.

It's not that Melissa's daddy is my favorite. It's just that Jeff is my only son. And he married Bernice, who's a nice girl, though she should treat my son with more respect. I'm proud of her being a teacher. My daughter-in-law the teacher. And Jeff likes things I like. Books and family history. And he stayed close, too, like his father.

Not like Charlene. I knew when she came home from college that first time she'd never come home again. Her eyes ashine when she talked about her friend from New York and her friend from Louisville and town this and town that. Should have made her go to school in Osierville, but the principal got her that scholarship at UK. She's not happy. I wonder what that medicine is she takes. Something for my swelled head, she said, trying to make a joke out of it. I hated it when she dropped out of school and married Bob. His mother coming to the wedding in her fur coat and earrings and picking at the little sandwiches Tessie and her cousin made out of Wonder Bread and cucumbers from the garden.

Tessie and her English novels. Miss my baby. Married the minute she got out of high school, and now she has four children. They're so poor and Floyd lost his job at the mine. Living over there in Johnson County. That rattletrap pickup won't last much longer, and then how will I see them, with Orson sick? Are the kids getting enough to eat? They look too pale, and Sandra has that cough.

Charlene's two boys look healthy enough. When I see them. This is the first weekend they've come in two, maybe three months. Never thought I'd appear "funny" to one of my own grandchildren. What Richard said to Hazlett in the backyard. "Gramma's funny about sex and stuff like that." Because I wouldn't let them watch that movie on TV the week that Charlene and Bob went vacationing in Bermuda. (I thought for a while they'd managed to make up, but Char says no, it didn't work.) When he was a little fellow, Hazlett loved me. His other grandma bought him that bicycle that he's too young for.

Charlene used to say "Oh Mother" in that tone. She was ashamed of her daddy's joking, too, I could tell. No more. She's swung the other way. Hallelujah. Bob would come in and sit down in front of the TV unless Jeff was here to talk sports with him. Never said more than two words to Orson. Wouldn't eat chicken and dumplings and picked at everything else, unless I made that beef roast Charlene gave me the recipe for. I don't like my son-in-law, Lord forgive me, and I'm glad they're separated. I didn't like the way he treated my daughter, like she was hired help. Yes he did. And I don't like the way he treats his children, giving them what they shouldn't have, too much *stuff*, and not giving them all the things they should have, like a few rules and maybe a church to go to. He can keep his money. She might divorce him, and I wouldn't care. Good thing Brother Johnson can't hear me say that.

When Char was two and crying with the toothache. We couldn't afford a dentist. Orson went out in the middle of the summer night and made a fire between the stones where we heated wash water in that burnt old tub. He went out in the dark on the hill and gathered dead wood while I worried about him getting snake bit, and he brought in the warm wood ashes to tamp in her tooth. It worked right off. They say it'll rot the teeth, though.

Fergus is the only adult I know who has perfect teeth, that devil. Beautiful Fergus, yes, he still is. That blond hair (with a triangle of gray on his right temple) ashine and the curly, short beard and those purple-blue eyes. (And, yes, his shoulders that move like water flowing and that long, lean backside.) Like an angel from above. Lucifer. That day by the spring upon the hill he came upon me and said what a lucky man Orson was. He carried my buckets of water down the hill and asked after Daddy and Mommy and said don't the honeysuckle smell good this year. He pushed back my hair. Washed in spring light. I looked into his purple eyes. Just then Mommy came out of the house, thank God, and he went away. I never told Orson. Nothing to tell.

Light and dark, Orson and Fergus. They fit together when you see them. My husband tall and dark and not too handsome but sweet, funny eyes, yes. They'll be fixing a truck or fishing or drinking together. Orson gets all silly with whisky but Fergus gathers into himself, ready to spring. He asked Orson if he could help with the bills last month. Orson said no, he told me, glad I bet to be able to say something good about Fergus.

We were at Sunday dinner when Orson told me that, and that Sunday we were alone. I always like family coming around on Sunday afternoons and we all sit in the front room with the TV silent and talk about the people we know and the people we used to know and what are things coming to now when they're stealing flowers off the graveyards.

Fergus comes from a cabin up Shady Hollow, a place respectable people don't hang around to this day. He was an only child. His daddy was a bootlegger that died when Fergus was twelve. His mother went to the crazy house in Lexington for a while, where Uncle Benjamin is. Fergus made do young. He's got charm, that's the word, and he's loving to them he loves. That being his mother and Orson.

I asked my husband, "Do you think he's got a good heart, Orson?"

He paused. "No, Sarah, I can't rightly say he has."

"Then why do you like him?" I asked. I was young.

"Just do," Orson said and spoke of other things.

I think Fergus is Orson's shadow. He's Orson's freedom from me and the children and the church I finally got him to join and from his own family. Freedom from the light.

Well, Fergus just got out of prison now, more's the pity, after shooting his cousin over that silly girl in the tavern. They say there'd been bad blood between them ever since his cousin's father took Fergus and his mother in for a few months. I hoped Fergus'd stay shut up. God forgive me, I guess. I think he touched Charlene where he shouldn't that day. She never would talk about it again. I made sure he was never alone with the girls after that. I should have told Orson, but I was afraid of what he might do. Or mightn't.

If Orson hadn't taken over the store, he could've made a living at building things. His hands helping Elswick fix that old wagon. I handed them the tools. Then Orson's cousin Elsie asked him to help her and Junior build a house and it turned out good. And it was good. Like everything Orson does turns out good.

Orson. Summer walking down Bear Hollow together, a tall, thin boy like my Cherokee great-great-granddaddy must've been. He was so funny that I forgot to watch out because he was a boy. The next year, when Orson was building a house for one of the Joneses and fell over that loose plank and broke his leg, Fergus finished Orson's job for him. Slowly, carefully, taking Orson's instructions. Wouldn't take no money for it. "Got plenty of greenbacks, buddy of mine." Jeff says Fergus has been peddling marijuana for years. And maybe worser stuff.

First time I'd ever been kissed standing under the sycamore tree down by Sarvis Creek. Cool brown water rippling by and Orson's warm lips. I kissed him back then. Only man who ever kissed my lips except for Daddy when I was little, I suppose. (And Fergus, that time in the kitchen. I pushed him away, away before I found myself kissing him back. Heat there. The hot stove and his hard, hot arms.) I've tried to be a good wife. Sometimes I think the Bible's been the ruination of us. Blasphemy. Melissa probably wouldn't think so. A child, and me taking her to church because mostly, most of the time, I think it's safer. God is a jealous god.

Orson doesn't think so. "Okay, honey, maybe you're right," he said, clutching at my arm in the hospital. "Tell Henry and Bill to come pray over me." (I felt like I was forcing medicine down his throat, the way I did to the kitten that time and it died.) He said Henry and Bill, not "Brother Lyman" and "Brother Johnson." I know he joined the church for me. He likes the singing, though, always did. Is he saved if he did it for me? Would God care? I can't afford to take the chance he don't. I have been of little faith.

But love the world you made, yes, Lord, the green hills circling around, the blue sky singing on that day when I thought my first baby was going to kill me. Lord, I don't want to go, I prayed. And he answered my prayer. Charlene. My oldest, yes, gone from me. Big in my womb that summer and Orson and me fighting. The mines went bust, too, and people were asking for credit at the store. Orson giving it to them. Jolene's Mary coming to stay with us. Just a little thing then. She tended the garden and cleaned the house. Hot July day. My water broke and I didn't know what was happening. Mary running barefoot to get old Rachel. Laughed about it afterward. Said she stepped on a big black snake and just kept on running. Rachel came on her mule, Mary up behind her. I thought I was going to die.

Darcy Anne Titwell. Just look at her over there looking at Orson. She really is. When I come out on the front porch after we got back from Lexington and the veterans' hospital, there she was. I couldn't believe my eyes.

"How's he doing?" she asked.

"You mean Orson?"

She flushed. "I was going to town to get some paint for Luellen and thought I'd just run over and see how he was."

"What's it to you?" I wanted to say. I made up my mind and said instead, "I was just going to sit here with a cup of coffee. Want to have some with me?"

She started to say no but said yes instead. I thought of Orson's jokes about moving up in the world. Marrying one of the Titwell girls. Now, that would've been up. I've seen her watch him every time she's been in our vicinity. We hemmed and hawed over the coffee, got nothing said. Funny, she doesn't strike me as the tongue-tied kind. Orson and she always say hello like two people who once knew each other well. I wonder what once went on between them.

My children's father, that tall, thin boy I grew up with, kissing me under the sycamores.

Tessie and Floyd are already at the house. Tessie will be stringing the beans and peeling the potatoes. Jeff and Bernice and Melissa will come after the reception, and Jeff and Floyd will go look at the garden while Bernice and Melissa help Tessie. Charlene's boys will be running in and out, whooping, playing. By the time dinner is almost ready, Char will forget to just look on and we'll talk about how things used to be. We'll sit in the front room then with the television off and talk about who's living and who's dying while the big white moon pulls the mountain on up to heaven.

CHARLENE

Sunlight flickers on the wall. My thoughts expand and flow out beyond the preacher's voice, beyond the still face of my father, beyond my mother's unshed tears. A faint echo of the voices beseeches God be with us. The world-swayed sunlight flickers like the candle flame in that painting by Gerhard Richter. (I had left the boys with Bob at his cousin's and gone to the museum alone. The little sign accompanying the painting spoke of the flame of the spirit.) The flame is for me a desire for changeless beauty, a closure not unlike the finality of sex. Yet flame alone is insufficient. We also need the baptismal waters, the immersion in life and death. The cool, sweet holler where Tessie and I used to play on summer afternoons.

I know my father's going to die. Daddy's going to die, and I'm thinking of divorcing my husband, and I'll be left alone with these two boys of mine and the threat of the voices. If he doesn't try to get custody—oh God, I couldn't stand that. He could use my condition. But most likely he'd pay guilt money. Doing it to his secretary. That's about how much imagination he has. Bob aspires to a good corporate life: weekdays, evenings, and weekends. Will I divorce him? Shall I divorce him?

And yet how patient he was when I broke, when the voices told me to run away and I got on a Greyhound and went from Lexington to Cincinnati. I told Mommy on the phone that some people had promised me a new life in Cincinnati, and she was afraid I meant a man, and I said no, Mommy, not a man, just some people I know, because how could I explain about the voices? I already had asked Bob the night before if he could hear them speaking and he looked at me, pinching his nose, and said he couldn't. "What about the boys?" Mommy pled, and I replied, "They'll be better off without me for a while." I went to the only hotel I knew in Cincinnati, where Bob and I had stayed one weekend.

When I called him and told him I'd be home in a few days probably, he got out of me where I was and the voices told me I had to move on. I repacked my clothes neatly, neatly, and called United Airlines about going to Chicago. Chelsea, my roommate in my senior year at UK, lived there. She had gone on to graduate school at the University of Chicago and then had moved in with a fellow student from the English Department. They opened a café near the university and it became a student hangout. Chelsea has never finished her Ph.D. and tells me frequently in her letters what a relief it has been to forget about it. At that time, she and Lawrence were thinking about getting married and having a child before it was too late, which they have done.

"*You make the marriage and child shtick sound so rewarding,*" she ended one letter to me, and I knew she hadn't been reading between the lines. I had been lying to myself as well, painting myself into a corner. Gradually I had realized Bob was being unfaithful. My existence teetered on the brink of his indifference. Of *my* indifference, which I could not admit. I was supposed to love only one man in this life. That was my story and I was sticking to it.

I called Chelsea and told her I needed to get away from Bob for a few days. I did not tell her about the voices that were skittering on the staircase and hanging suspended from the night sky. "Don't call Bob," they said. "Don't talk to the boys. Don't call home. They'll be in danger, too, if you do, if you do, if you do." They liked to repeat themselves.

"By all means come to us," Chelsea said in her best Chicago voice. "We have a guest room now." She sounded concerned, as though she knew there was something I wasn't telling her. As we rang off, I heard her voice directed toward someone else, Larry of course. I was too preoccupied with the voices to worry about whatever she might be telling him. Too preoccupied to worry about whether she was worrying about me. About the worry I might be causing Bob, who is, after all, a man not devoid of feeling.

I had never been in a large airport before and the belt walkways at O'Hare seemed surreal. There was a long tangle of neon lights above one stretch. It seemed as noisy as the voices, which were now chanting that help was at hand, but they didn't sound like they meant it. A cab took me to Hyde Park. It was four o'clock on an August afternoon and I could see the heat screaming off the eclectic strings of homes and businesses along the expressway. Then we were on Lake Shore Drive and the beauty of the lake struck me like a high trumpet note, the leafy splendor of isolated trees in the lakeside park.

Heat danced about the cab as we made our way through the solid homes and wilted greenery of Chelsea's neighborhood. "This is it, lady," the driver said, pulling up before dingy brick. He had been trying to make conversation for the past hour. I grabbed my suitcase and overnight bag and went through the freshly painted white door. There were dim tiles in the foyer and a seascape on the wall. How crazy to have a seascape in a city with a lake like that. I pressed their apartment buzzer, which was flanked by their two surnames. Chelsea's voice came raspingly over the old intercom. "Wait there, dear, and I'll bring the elevator down." I wondered when I had become Chelsea's "dear." Disheveled, in a stale dress, the wary traveler

greeted her host, her sister of yore who now had other alle-
giances. Chelsea hugged me and said "Dear" again. I broke into
desperate tears. She got me upstairs, where the air conditioner
laid a sweaty cool on my skin. "What did he do?" she asked at
once, taking my bags and motioning to a low white couch. I
fell awkwardly upon it, a hillbilly come to rest. "What on earth
did he do, Charlene?" Kentucky had returned to her voice like
a solace. But I kept my voices secret all the same. Instead, I
told her about Bob's secretary. "That bastard," she said, with
all the proper feeling in her voice, but complacency was there
too. Larry had evidently been behaving himself, as we say in
the hills and just about anywhere else women congregate.

Chelsea said, "Stay with us a few days and decide what
you're going to do," and Larry was concerned and patient.
They took me to an Italian restaurant and for dessert we
had what they swore was the world's best tiramisu. High on
two glasses of house wine, I ate all of my rich dessert while
they talked about national politics and the new restaurant on
57th Street. The voices disappeared for a while and in their
place was an empty black hole. So I knew I had to get back
to Lexington. "Well, if you really feel that way," Chelsea said
with relief and concern mingled. "It might be best, dear." They
took me to the airport, where I waited all night.

I returned to Cincinnati and checked back into the hotel,
and Bob found me there ripping the phone from the wall and
brought me home, and his sister called a psychiatrist. Bob
wanted to sit in on my sessions, but Dr. Weinstein said no. I
could see how that bothered Bob. A whole secret part of my
life that he wasn't in on. Bob likes to be in control. For the
month that the medicine was taking effect, he got his sister to
stay with us during the day, for fear I'd hurt myself, for fear
I'd hurt the boys. Mommy would have come if I'd asked her, if
I'd told her, but I couldn't deal with that.

Bob would come in from work and hug me gingerly and
then the boys and help his sister get supper. Finally, I could

tell the half-truth: "Okay, I'm all right now." "Why are you still taking those pills, then?" "Oh, I have to keep on them for a long time." But nothing is forever. When I die, I won't need to take the blue and purple pills anymore. Dr. Weinstein says perhaps even before that, though we've tried it once and it was no good. The voices came back after a few weeks. He says I'm lucky to have these new pills. They may damage my heart but in the meantime they give it leeway. I laugh, I cry. I'm not on such a tight leash anymore.

It's not like I love Bob now, if ever I did. Dazzled by his upscale intonations and by a certain pucker in his upper lip when he smiled. Poor Bob. You can't really blame him for preferring his secretary. I wonder if he patronizes her the way he does me. Mommy doesn't think I know this about Bob. I've seen her look at him appraisingly and then give me a pitying look. Dad always has his best-behaved face on. What they don't know is that, before Bob, Edgar had asked me to marry him. He was bright and warm of heart and bumbling and he meant to go back south to his home county and practice medicine. I couldn't forgive him the bumbling and I didn't want to leave the big city. Well, there you are. The heart has its preferences, and it's a wise woman who learns first that the heart is often a fool and, second, that it must nonetheless be obeyed. Fortunately, the heart can be fickle, and I no longer think I love Bob.

Mommy thinks Bob has ruined me for my own kind (or was that UK?). Neither fish nor fowl nor good red herring. What does Daddy think? I don't know, and he's too polite to tell me. I've got the best-mannered parents in the world and Bob can't see it because they both say "ain't" sometimes and like fried chicken and fried okra. It hasn't helped us that I too like fried chicken and fried okra. The boys do, too, and sometimes I fry chicken for Sunday dinner. They love Mom's blackberry cobbler also, and when they were younger they loved going down home. (Hazlett still does.) Now they attend ritzy private schools and their friends sneer at hillbillies.

I know Bob is ashamed of me. I've got the right vocabulary and I've learned how to play his games, but what Bob when he's angry calls my Appalachian whine is there good and strong. Give me a week down home and I can say "ain't" as well as anybody and have been known to call a paper bag a poke and an industrious person smart. That's from Dad. Mommy got a little gentrified early on. Grandma Alseck was a lady, and she learned proper English from *her* mother, who was a schoolteacher, who learned it from *her* mother, who married a farmer and had sons who were coal miners and daughters who married coal miners, but she made sure that her children were gentry. Mommy is definitely a lady. And she's never been known to wear a pair of pants except at berry-picking time. She buys fine cotton and makes her own dresses, plain and well-fitting, pastel and ladylike. And my sister Tessie is a lady, for all that she wears pants most of the time. Me, I'm not so sure.

I never take the Mountain Parkway south from Lexington unless the weather turns out to be bad. Instead, we travel winding mountain roads beneath overlapping trees: to my right, the brown glint of a creek recently rained into. Before Bob and I opted for a trial separation, the boys would grow querulous on the back seat, and Bob was no doubt stiffly wishing that he were on the golf course (or with his secretary). Now Hazlett sits beside me up front while Richard is restless in the back. The three of us play games such as counting the horses; white horses thirty whole points. Until recently on these roads, I only slumped a little inside, while on the outside I maintained my patrician look and speech that belonged to our Federal-style house and comported with our standing in the world. More and more, though, I have slumped on the outside also. Partly this has been a political statement aimed at my husband, partly a pedagogical one aimed at my sons too late, too late, and partly it is the inner necessity of my new-found me-ness.

This church to which we have come with Mommy since I can remember, first at the old building, which, like Mom, I prefer. We are barely perched on this hill. A few years ago that fool Lane Gorman cut the timber on his property up above and the soil is running downhill, slowly, surely It has already reached the graveyard above the church. Last spring, part of the road up to the church washed out. They had to shore it up with rocks. Cousin Jervis is officiating over Emile's marriage to Bertha. I am sure he would rather be preaching from the Book of Job, which he does in nearly every sermon since he lost his two boys in the Vietnam War and his wife died of cancer, though everybody says she really died of grief.

I had a vision once when I was a teenager. The skin of the earth on the mountains loose and ready to be shaken away at the slight jarring, carrying houses, people with it. There would be nothing left but rock. That was the spring Fergus pulled me aside into the undergrowth. He kissed me and ran his hands over me and said, "I'll let you go, little bird, because of who your Daddy is. Don't you tell him now, or I'll have to kill him." For a long time I wanted him to touch me again and that was the worst part. I shared with my father a leaning toward Fergus, on my part the sheer physical charm of the man and that laugh that has no holds barred, a sickness I could not expel. An underbrush of laurel, thick and smothering, and below Fergus the creek that runs past the house. Sarvis Creek coming off of the mountain, which is steep and green with a gray cliff near the top and in that lime-green spring was dotted with the pure white blossoms of the sarvis (serviceberry, they call it elsewhere, or sugar plum) tree. Instead of going back on the road, I slipped into the creek and ran, water ballooning out my socks and sloshing in my shoes. "Whatever got into you?" Mommy asked and I cried but I was afraid to tell her because she might tell Daddy and Fergus would kill him. She looked up and saw Fergus coming toward the house and her face tightened in the way it always did when he came around. "Get on in the house, Charlene," she said and I gladly did so. She came, too, and closed the door. He did not stop but went on by, whistling in the way that he has. I still feel a darkness near the bone when Fergus is in the vicinity. He is at the wedding today, sitting at the back on the other side, his gaze fixed on Daddy like a cat watching a bird. I have wondered if he ever had been at Mommy, too.

But not Tessie. My sister Tessie is wholesome and sturdy and full of light. I remember the first time I came home from UK and Tessie came out to meet me, an apron around her waist and a blackberry stain where she had rubbed her jelly-making finger along her cheek, and I thought, she is good, that's the word for Tessie, good. Tessie has joined the Methodists, to which her Floyd has belonged since childhood, but I know they don't go to services more than two or three times a year. Tessie doesn't need to go to church. She probably has dispensation from upstairs to be about her business, which is largely coping with poverty in a large-handed kind of way. When I go visit Tessie in Johnson County—Hazlett likes to come with me, to play with his cousins—she plucks this nothing and that from her pantry shelves and cooks a delicious meal. Afterward we go sit on the back porch and talk about family. Our family and her family and my boys, never anything much about Bob. Tessie's four children are much better behaved than my two and they seem happy and pretty much loyal to the family concept. When Floyd is out of work, as he is now, the family gets by with their garden stuff and the chickens and corn from their field. My sister's husband is quick and intense and acts as though my sister provides his natural environment. Sine qua non.

I was the bright one, but Tessie—as a professor of mine said about my acquaintance with philosophy—knows enough for her purposes. Sweet Tessie with a will of iron and a heart of gold. Only clichés will serve. I like Floyd, too. Never once has he flirted with me or remarked upon the absences of my husband. Mommy gave Mamaw Wright's churn to Tessie, who coveted it not as a collectible but as a serviceable item. It sits by Tessie's fireplace, the white cloth that covers it secured by a strip of yellow fabric. The new wooden dasher made by Floyd hangs over the fireplace like a domestic replacement for the sword. Butter, not guns.

When did Floyd have the job in that two-bit mining operation owned by one of their neighbors? About five years ago. Part of the roof collapsed, and a falling rock broke Floyd's shoulder and he was laid up for the best part of the winter. Daddy tried to help them out, but they wouldn't take more than the bare minimum. At least Floyd wouldn't. (Tessie would have taken it for the children.) The brakes went out on their old pickup, and Tessie would walk five miles in her threadbare coat to the store and back when they had to have groceries, taking the eldest boy, Martin, with her. Their youngest, Callie, developed what was probably pneumonia, but the doctor wouldn't come out without getting his pay. (Tessie walked to the store to call him.) My sister sat up three days and nights holding Callie's head over steam, making her drink ginger tea, keeping her warm and dry, and rubbing Vicks on her chest. Martin learned how to cook pinto beans and Irish potatoes and how to make gravy for breakfast. He's no hand at biscuits, Tessie says, hard as rocks. So she told him what ingredients to use for cornbread, and they had cornbread and gravy for breakfast. Since they don't have a phone, the rest of us didn't know about it until later. The children of the poor grow up young.

Thank God Daddy's a veteran or Mommy and he would get shorn of all their worldly goods. First there was the operation, then the radiation and chemotherapy, and the visits to this doctor and that, and the medicines. He was able to keep our land and the store, and there is family close by, most importantly Jeff, dear old thing, brother mine, but Tessie and Floyd are pretty much alone over there in Johnson County.

Some of Floyd's family live over there, but they are poorer yet.

I know Daddy didn't want Tessie to marry Floyd. I heard him and Mommy arguing about it one night. Bob and I had come down for the weekend. We had quarreled ourselves and I couldn't sleep. When I went to the kitchen to get a drink of water, I heard my parents through the screen door, on the back porch half-whispering.

"He'll be like my cousin Willard. Deeper and deeper in debt and one day he'll walk off and leave Tessie."

"Now, Orson, Floyd ain't like Willard at all. He's got his piece of land and he works when he can get work."

"Look at that daddy of his. Drunk ten months of the year."

"Floyd doesn't touch the stuff, Orson, and you know it." And then Mommy got to *her* big worry. "You want Tessie to marry off like Charlene did?"

Through the screen door I saw Daddy's shoulders slump.

When I pulled into the yard yesterday morning, above the boys' clamor I saw them in tableau: Daddy sitting in the slightly rusting lawn chair—his face as pale as skim milk and the dip of solid white hair—thin and desiccated now, the olive-green shadows around his eyes, his socks loose on spindly legs, the convexity of his back, concavity of his chest. And Mommy, Mommy who is always so *correct*, wisps of hair escaping from her bun, a faintly crazed look in her eyes, and a tomato stain on her fine cotton dress. I could have shrieked out. These could be the parents of a daughter who heard voices.

***

Once in my high school years, I went into town with a classmate who had a car and money to spend. She was treating me to dinner at the Stetson Steakhouse. I didn't tell my parents that. After dinner, we strolled down Locust Street beneath what to us were the bright lights. Suddenly Janice Sue said, "There's your daddy, Charlene." And there he was, with two other men. One was Sheriff Corrigan, who once in a while comes out to the house and sits on the porch with Daddy. The other one was Fergus. My father looked rumpled and loose in a way I had never seen. Fergus had a hand on his shoulder and one on the sheriff's, which I found interesting, since Corrigan had arrested Fergus a number of times for this reason and that. Fergus was speaking and the others were nodding their heads and laughing. They looked as though they were sharing some unsavory secret. "Want to go over and say hello?" Janice Sue asked curiously. "No," I said, my heart thumping for fear Daddy would see me, "let's go on to the movie."

He has been a kind father, always somewhat remote and yet lovable. His remoteness is something other than the separateness a family feels toward the breadwinner who spends his day at the office or in the mine or laying bricks. It suggests a preoccupation with matters that are alien to the rest of us. Orson Caskill is generally considered to be a good man, his acquaintanceship with Fergus some mere whim or peccadillo allowable to someone who adheres in important respects to the straight and narrow. Even though, unlike Mommy, he has never been a churchgoer until now, when fear must surely be his driving force. I wish that I hadn't had to see him and Mommy that way when they were staying with us in Lexington and he was getting treated. Out of their element, out of Osier County—and him half out of life. They were diminished because there was no way for them to express their lives. Bob didn't help, of course. But, worse, I didn't either. But, look, they're back here, stronger than ever in that way. Burnished with pain and the dealing with it, the refusal of it.

***

After the pills began to work, Bob and I decided on this separation. It was obvious that he was torn about the boys. He didn't really want Richard and Hazlett around cluttering up his romance with Sally, but he really was afraid that I was in no shape to be looking after them. I talked to Betty about this. Another UK roommate. All those weekends I spent in her parents' backyard in Lexington shooting baskets. Betty had gone on to get a graduate degree at Morehead and is teaching in the education department there.

She now has a big house in a complex a mile or so out of Morehead. "I'm just rattling around in here," she said to me. "Why don't you and the boys come and stay with me for a while? There's lots of room, and you could take a course or two. Be good for you." Betty is a sweet friend and it was far enough away from Bob and yet close enough for him to see the boys. "Betty will be there, too," I told Bob, and he was relieved but said we must ask the boys. Richard wanted to stay with his father. My sweet little boy who was no longer little and who had been scared silly by my illness. He is thin and dark, not like either of his parents, and already he is impatient with me, having picked that up early from his father. Thank God he is visiting with Hazlett and me this weekend.

Hazlett, only four, said he'd like to go with Mommy. (In this choice of appellation for myself, I had overruled Bob, who wanted the children to call me Mother as they called him Father.) My youngest sits beside me now (Richard sitting beyond him at a metaphorical distance), leaning trustfully against me, his eternally tousled hair damp around the edges from a late shampoo. We three played blindman's buff last night with my Mommy and Daddy. The sound of Hazlett's chortles. Richard's disdain.

My unhappiness about Richard's deciding to live with his father (for of course Bob said he must, a flash of triumph in the eyes) was compounded by my guilt: guilt that I had allowed Richard to become so thoroughly his father's son, guilt about my dislike of my son's conformity to his peer group and his avarice for material things.

So Hazlett and I took off for Morehead in the SUV, our

transient belongings crowded in the back. Every other weekend Bob brings Richard and the next weekend I take Hazlett
to Lexington. When I bring Hazlett into Lexington, I take
Richard for an outing. He is getting to like me again, but I
think he despises me a little as well.

Last fall, I signed up for that creative writing course at
Morehead and for the one on twentieth-century art. I have
been playing hooky from life, and Betty has aided and abetted
me. We took turns in the winter cooking competitive meals
in her spacious kitchen, our supplies augmented by good-
ies brought back from Lexington. (Morehead groceries tend
toward the downhome.) My courses were chosen with an eye
to Betty's free time, so she could look after Hazlett while I
was in class. Hazlett soon became attached to her. Betty's boy-
friends make big over him, as we say in the hills. All those
male buddies she has, and the steady boyfriend who works at
computers in Lexington and comes to collect her on Saturday
mornings.

Some weekends, then, when I have returned from
Lexington, having left Hazlett there, I am alone at El Mansion,
as we have taken to calling Betty's place. My sickness is not
bothering me nearly as much now, except for the pointless
anxiety and the brief flush of voices at a moment. On these
weekends that I am alone, I feel beatifically lost in space. I
go into the cramped, shabby town and it widens out to welcome me. On Sunday morning, especially, I go in to breakfast
at the Maple Leaf Grill. Eggs and ham and biscuit and gravy,
all prepared in the best downhome way, and orange juice and
coffee. They know me there now and pass remarks about the
weather and whatever might be going on in town that weekend. The faces of other regulars have become familiar, and
sometimes Ray, who works in a lumber mill, or Georgia, who
is a substitute teacher, engages me in conversation. They both
come from deep in the hills, too. Georgia used to be a teacher
in Letcher County but left when her husband was killed in a

mining accident. Ray came up from Johnson County to see his young cousin who was attending the university; he heard about a job at the lumber mill and stayed. They both say they are homesick, but Georgia has acquired a man friend in town and Ray is making good money as a foreman.

Almost a year has gone by in this fashion. Bob and I seem no closer to making a decision. The boys appear resigned to their respective situations. Last fall I made some near-friends in the creative writing class, which was taught by a local celebrity who had gone elsewhere and come back "too big for his britches," as one of my new acquaintances said. Who was it that asked me if I would like to join the writing group that met once a week?

I pulled up outside that restaurant/beer joint and a very tall woman and a short, skinny man went in ahead of me and sat down at the table in the back. "I'm Al," the short man said, puffing on an unfiltered cigarette. "I'm writing a novel. And this is Hannah. She writes poetry." Hannah, a blonde with beautiful white skin and a sharp nose, tossed her head and said nothing. "I write poetry, too," I offered apologetically.

Hannah sniffed. "Little lyric gems, I bet," she said.

"Narrative poetry *cum* Ashbery," I said in my best Lexingtonian, Federal-style-house voice.

Other people came in, among them the fateful Randall Henry and Winona Crysler. Randall had given Winona a ride all the way up from Johnson County in his old green car. Randall, about my age, had a tawny beard and light blue eyes. He looked like Fergus. The resemblance jolted me, and I gave him a cold hello as introductions were made.

Winona and I quickly developed a friendship. She was in her sixties, a small, plain woman with iron-gray hair and sweet brown eyes. She told me, months later, that she had been the top student in her high school classes, graduated from a community college, then left her parents behind and moved to Philadelphia. ("Why Philadelphia?" "Because the Liberty Bell was there," she said, grinning.) Her impeccable grammar and spelling ability got her a job in a printing concern and from there, several years later, she had moved on to a newspaper, where she had eventually become a reporter on the city beat. Her mother died and her visits home became more and more infrequent. Then her father developed cancer of the colon, and she had thrown over her life in Philadelphia and moved home to take care of him. Ten years of that.

"How could you take moving back, Winona? All that movement and excitement and then to come home. Didn't it seem narrow? Weren't you lonely?"

"Yes, it did seem narrow, and at first I was very lonely. Even lonelier," she grimaced, "than I had been in the city. And taking care of Daddy was no picnic. He was so dependent on me, and you know how unpleasant colon cancer can be."

"Why haven't you gone back to Philadelphia?"

"Daddy left me the house, and it's not a bad house, and it has a large garden and a stretch of woods out back and I can watch the sunrise over the hill in the morning. So I thought if I could get a job, I might as well stay home. Maybe I'd find a way not to be lonely. So I went over to the local newspaper and showed them some of my work. I lucked out. They were expanding out into the county and they needed an extra editor." Winona writes stories about her hometown. In their depiction of characters bent by circumstance, they are not unlike Sherwood Anderson's *Winesburg, Ohio*, but the nimbus of light and redemption that surrounds her people is something particular to herself alone. I looked at my artificial poems and was ashamed.

Winona had never been married—"not for lack of trying," she would say humorously—and yet I came to feel that there was a kind of inviolable integrity to her, a basic feminism that did not lend itself well to marriage. I said something of the kind to her once and she turned a very real anger on me. Two or three love affairs had come her way, not in Johnson

County or even in Kentucky, but Out There. Mostly she had been alone.

One weekend when Bob had the boys in Lexington, she invited me down to see her place and to sit and talk, something we did a great deal of in the Maple Leaf Grill. It was January now. Christmas had come and gone, an uneasy Christmas spent in Lexington, where Bob and I took separate bedrooms and Hazlett cried because Betty was not there and Richard looked as though he was afraid to be glad I was there. I eased the SUV onto the Mountain Parkway and suddenly the air was full of possibilities. The bare tree limbs sang hosanna on the mountains. I was going in the general direction of home, but for the first time I was not going as a daughter. Often when I get excited now, the voices materialize, so to speak, but that day they were entirely silent. On that day, the power of the wheel was almost an aphrodisiac.

At around 2:00, I drove past Winona's frozen flower beds into the little bay beside her white frame house, probably a century old but sturdy. There was Victorian fretwork at the porch's upper edge. Huddled in her maroon down coat, Winona sat in the porch swing, which was suspended from four shiny chains.

"Come on in," she said, getting up and opening the door into a well-lit living room. A new-looking flowered couch took up a great deal of space in the small room. Behind the couch, each window was flanked by a planter's stand, tiered with blooming things. A steady fire bloomed in the wide fireplace. "No central heating," Winona said. "There's a wood stove in the kitchen and I keep a heater in my bedroom." I was glad of the couch's proximity to the fireplace. Central heating can make a sissy out of you in no time flat.

We went out to look at the great oak tree in the backyard and to wander among the frozen weeds in the garden. Afterward, Winona made a pot of coffee and we settled ourselves on the plump-cushioned couch and a matching armchair. In the middle of our conversation about the holidays just past, Winona said, "Randall's coming to join us at dinner." I was not happy about that. "It seemed like a good chance for us downhome folk to get together," Winona added.

Randall looked very large in the small living room. Winona hugged him and took his coat.

"You look like someone I know," I blurted out, thinking of Fergus.

"Somebody respectable, I hope," he said easily, starting to sit down.

"You and Charlene come on out in the kitchen with me," Winona commanded.

There was a strong fire in the wood stove. The stovepipe was looking a little red. Winona's spaghetti sauce sat on a side burner, bubbling softly. She poured glasses of cheap red wine and put the spaghetti water on to boil.

"Is he?" Randall asked.

"Is who what?" Winona countered.

"Is the person I look like respectable?" he asked again, still looking at Winona.

"Funny you should ask," I said, and then, feeling somehow reckless, found myself telling them about Fergus. Not about the time he kissed me and felt me up. Not about his closeness to Daddy. But all the rest about Fergus that I knew.

"Jesus," Randall commented, now looking at me. "I hope he ain't kin."

"You should write about him," Winona said, filling the salad bowls.

"Not without she writes about me, too," Randall said, laughing. "I'm his twin."

"My hero," Winona drawled, reaching over and ruffling his hair.

I felt shut out from their easy camaraderie, from their obvious attachment. "How did you get interested in the coal industry?" I asked Randall, thinking of his dissertation, a small section of which he had read at a writing group session.

"My granddaddy and my daddy and several of my uncles worked in the mines. I tried it myself but it turned out I was afraid of the dark." He was now teaching in a county high school.

I looked at his tawny, laughing face. "You don't look like you'd be afraid of much," I said.

"As always, appearances are deceiving," he replied. "It's easy to laugh now. I'm not down there anymore."

"What about your brothers?" I asked.

"Don't have any. No sisters, either."

"Like me," Winona said.

"Well, it wasn't deliberate with my parents," Randall went on. "Mom had to have an operation after I was born. That's how I got to college. Nobody to share the money with."

"All three of us come from small families," Winona said. "Charlene has just got a sister and a brother."

"What do they do? Come to think about it, what do you do?" he asked me.

I looked around at Winona's well-lit kitchen and at the two of them, relaxed in their chairs, at home. "I'm a housewife," I said, "but I'm taking a break from it right now."

Basking in Winona's glow, we enjoyed her pleasant spaghetti sauce and the store-bought apple pie that accompanied the rich, strong coffee. After a while, Randall said he had to go grade papers. As he put his coat on, our eyes met.

***

Sitting here watching Emile and Bertha's excitement on this otherwise quiet Sunday morning, surrounded by the familiar, once again relinquishing Randall, as I have done a thousand times, I look over at my brother Jeff. He doesn't look like he's paying much attention to the wedding. If Tessie is the good one in the family, Jeff is the passionate one. He's crazy about Bernice, crazy about the Democratic Party, crazy about Mommy, and crazy about his daughter. With Daddy it's another matter. They're real close when it comes to doing things, but I've never seen them share an emotional moment. Jeff doesn't have time for much of anything or anybody other than his family. He cannot stand Bob, who cordially dislikes him, too. And I'm forgetting that guitar of his; he plays it every chance he gets. But mostly he works in the store.

On one Saturday evening, Bob and I were talking about the property Bob had purchased in Menifee County. We were planning eventually to build a vacation home there. "Oh, and Jeff can help build it," I said impulsively. That's another thing Jeff's good at. He learned it from Daddy.

"I've already mentioned it to a firm in Lexington," Bob said stiffly.

"Just as well," Jeff said. "I'm not innerested."

They'd stopped talking about the Wildcats by that time of the evening. The only safe topic.

***

At our next writing group meeting, Randall said that he would be visiting a Morehead friend over the weekend. "Mind if I join you for Sunday breakfast at the Maple Leaf?"

"I'm spending the weekend in Lexington."

"Will you be back by Sunday morning?"

"No."

He hesitated. "We could have Sunday dinner at the Ranchero."

I flushed. "I don't think so."

He tore a corner from a sheet of paper. "If you change your mind, you can reach me at this number."

"Okay," I told him, thinking that I wouldn't.

The flirtation, that humorous glint in the eye, that raised eyebrow.

Bob and I had an argument that weekend and when

Hazlett and I got back to Morehead I called the number. "Are you sure you want to do this?" Betty asked, putting a protective arm around Hazlett.

"I'm only going out to dinner," I said. Perhaps Randall said the same thing to his friends.

Our first topic of conversation was the writing group. Then we talked about Winona and then we talked about his dissertation. We were well into our steak and fries when Randall raised the specter of Fergus. "I knew a man like that," he said. "He was a state patrolman, though. Picked up me and my buddy on a marijuana charge."

"And did you have any?"

"Well, we'd just smoked a joint, but that wasn't why he was riled up. He'd been laying for my buddy."

"Why?"

"Grant's daddy had pistol-whipped him for cheating at cards."

"Why didn't he arrest Grant's daddy, then?"

"They were neither one supposed to be where they were. *Or* playing cards for money."

"Did you go to jail?"

"For one night. Grant had flipped the remainder of the joint a far distance, and we'd just smoked that one, which we got off my cousin, so there wasn't any evidence."

"Do you smoke a lot of marijuana?" I asked.

"No, not since I left high school. Smoked every chance I could get then, though."

"How come you decided to give it up?"

"Left home and didn't need it anymore. Didn't have the money to buy it anyhow in college. And afterward, well, I just didn't think it was a good thing."

"Fergus sells it. And worse stuff."

"Yeah, I know. You told us. Why do you mind so much about Fergus?"

I told him. He put his hand on top of mine and said,

"Bastard." As his hand had reached out, I expected to feel repulsed, but it wasn't like Fergus, not at all.

"And you look like him," I said.

"Well, I'm *not* him, Charlene."

"Why did you need marijuana while you were at home?"

"My mother didn't love me."

"No. Really."

"That *is* really. I got no warmth from her at all. When I was sick, my daddy took care of me."

"Did she work?"

"No. She took up with men, any kind of man, lots of men. Kept her pretty busy. They threw her out of the church. We kept the neighborhood in talk."

"How come your father didn't leave her?"

"To tell the truth, I don't know. He didn't even argue with her about it. I guess he loved her. Anyhow, I got to college, and after I almost flunked out, they sent me to a counselor, a psychologist."

I looked at his vulnerable eyes. "I'm seeing a psychiatrist now," I said.

"Why?"

I told him.

We kissed tenderly before I got out of his car back at Betty's. "Come down next weekend," he said urgently, and gave me his address, with directions.

But Wednesday night, Randall and Winona didn't come to the writing group. I called Winona the next day. "Terrible news about Randall's cousin," she said. "I'm covering the funeral for the paper."

"What happened?"

"He was working his usual shift at the mine. Whatever he had in his hand snapped a water hose. Its coupling was metal, don't you know, and it hit his neck so hard that it broke it."

"Was Randall close to him?"

"They used to hang out together in high school. The

cousin was a little older, and Randall looked up to him."

I called Randall. "Well, we used to be close," he said, "and I still liked him a lot. The funeral starts on Friday, and there'll be preaching for three days. Can you come the next weekend?"

"No, it's my weekend with the boys."

"Then the weekend after that."

I thought that now was the time to stop, but I said, "Let's talk about it the Wednesday before." I daydreamed about him constantly. I neglected my coursework, my poems, my son. When the second weekend came, I went to Johnson County.

***

Randall lived at the head of a holler. Its road was narrow and rocky, and the SUV seemed to hang over the side as it lurched its way upward, alongside the holler itself, its clear, thin water rushing over pebbles of all sizes and hues. I prayed that I wouldn't meet a car coming down and have to back my way out. I passed only one house as I ascended.

The holler opened up at the top into a large yard. Against the hill on the right was a line of hickory trees. Between the yard and the hill to the left was a long, narrow garden, two rows of brown cornstalks bent into the pitted snow. His snug garage and another outbuilding were painted green. The house itself was a log affair of the modern kind, the logs half black with creosote. There were no curtains at the windows, which gleamed in the late morning sun. Randall stood in the tidy doorway and watched me park the SUV in front of his garage. Then he came slowly to meet me. Nervously I praised his home. "Built this house myself," he said, "with a little help from my cousins and some instructions that I bought on the Internet. We'll have to be careful or it might tumble down." I obediently laughed.

The silence and the space and this stranger I had come to see. But it grew easier inside the small house. From the living room, which also served as his study and library, I could see along the hall to a dining room/kitchen. "I made that table," he said, his eyes following mine. I stood with my coat half off and looked. It was a round table, oak, with legs that looked a little narrow for its weight, and the chairs around it were the old cane-bottomed kind. "Did you make the chairs?" I asked.

"No, I'm not *that* good. Picked them up here and there and had them re-caned by old Silas Gurney over in Milltown. You can see they're all different from one another but they've all got seats with a checkerboard pattern. Silas did that by using new hickory bark for the light-colored weave and hickory bark he'd soaked in the creek for the dark weave. And look at this rocker over here, it's my favorite. Sassafras with walnut pegs."

I warmed to the enthusiasm in his voice. "I'm spending the night at Winona's," I said nervously, outrageously.

His hands paused on the Kentucky atlas that he was pulling out to show me. "Okay, but you've got to stay for supper," he said in a response that took account of the implications. "I got it all planned."

On that short, sun-filled afternoon, we talked, and before too long we kissed. At five o'clock he put his meatloaf in the oven. I peeled potatoes, and he prepared green beans with bacon grease the way Mommy does. We ate an early supper and did the dishes, and he kissed me lengthily. Then I went to Winona's, glad of a reprieve in which I thought I might gather my lyrical thoughts.

By April we were steady lovers. One Saturday afternoon in May, we went into town to pick up some groceries and ran into Jeff, who had come over to Johnson County to see an old high school buddy. I introduced Randall as an acquaintance from Morehead and made a point of lying to Jeff that I was staying at Winona's. Randall received a hard, wary look and gave a placating one in return. Jeff had certainly seen Randall's arm around my waist. Now he ignored Randall entirely and told me grimly to take care, his voice a warning. I flushed in spite of myself.

"He knows," I said to Randall when we got back in the SUV.

"Soon everybody will know now, won't they?" Randall replied, touching my cheek.

"Then I'll have to divorce Bob."

"Well, I hope so. You can't be married to two men at once in Kentucky," he said, looking sideways at me as he backed out. I saw the little scar beside his mouth turn red the way it did when something significant was going on. (He had been hit by a piece of flying debris during a thunderstorm.)

I kissed his shoulder, my mouth sensual against the rough fabric. We were silent for a while.

"I don't know if the boys will be happy down here," I said worriedly. "I know they wouldn't at first."

His hands tightened on the wheel. "Wouldn't it be best if Bob kept the boys?" he asked.

I drew away.

"I guess we could keep the little one," he added reluctantly, "and let the older boy stay with his dad, the way you fellows are handling it now." The little one, the older one.

"I want them both," I said. "I want to have your baby, too."

He shook his head violently. "I don't want to bring any children into this world," he said. "And there's your health to consider."

"You mean my *mental* health?"

"It has to be thought of."

"I can't live with that," I replied angrily.

"You see what a world we live in," he said mulishly. "There's enough poor babies in it already. And look at your kids. Living with half a family."

"We could make it a whole one."

"What about their dad?"

I left before dinner and returned to Morehead. I did not go to the writing group anymore. Winona was sympathetic but thought I should have enough backbone to stick with the writing group. I hoped half-heartedly that sooner or later Randall would call and we could just forget about marriage, forget about the future. But he did not. He's seeing someone else now, Winona tells me.

I can't wait any longer for Bob to make the decision. Or for my father to die. Daddy won't be any more troubled about a divorce than he has been by my marriage. Him and Mommy both. I've got to talk it out with Bob, to see if we can agree about the boys before we hire the lawyers. Though maybe he's already got a lawyer. Maybe he's planning to take the boys. Thank God I'm no longer seeing Randall. I've got to talk to Betty. If I can stay at Morehead and take education courses. I'd rather go to UK, but the money won't be there. And Bob might let me have the boys if I stay with Betty. But she may get married soon. And what would I do with Richard? He wouldn't be happy in Morehead.

Maybe I can get a job and take the courses at UK. Then we'd all be in Lexington and Bob could see the boys as often as he liked. Maybe he'll help pay for the courses. I wonder how often Bob would want to see his sons. I no longer think that I know my husband very well and I know he feels he never knew me. He told me so. (But I do know he'll be relieved never to have to come to Sarvis Creek anymore.)

Well, I'll be a teacher, then. Thanks to Bob, I saw a private psychiatrist, so I don't need to list my "condition." The boys are old enough now. Move out somewhere nice like Winchester and let Bob keep the Federal-style house, which I loved twice as much as Bob probably but which now gives me claustrophobia. I can bring my sons down home without his disapproving shadow. Perhaps it's not too late to teach Richard that he belongs here too.

Sunlight flickers on the wall, flames on familiar faces, forever lost, forever gained. The spirit of our lives moves me, moves me here. I am the prodigal child, Ishmael the wanderer come home to rest, to gather them about me as though I would never—but will always—let them go. My home holds me, immerses me in the baptismal waters, heals me.

JEFF

ernice is daydreaming about leaving again; leaving
Osier County, leaving Kentucky. She wants to move to
Ohio because she heard there are good jobs in Dayton.
How can I tell her that would be a kind of death for me, to
leave where I spent my childhood and the people I grew up
with, to leave the magic circle of the hills? There's not much
I can fault my wife about, nor do I want to, because I love
her even more than when I married her. All these years we've
spent together and the daughter we have raised. I hope Bertha
and Emile will be as happy as Bernice and I have been, and I'm
happy to be here for the wedding, Emile suited up and Bertha
glorious in white, just as it should be. But mostly I skip church.
If they'd just let me bring my guitar. If I could just play along
when they're singing "O Come, Angel Band" or "Just One Rose
Will Do." Too bad all the singing is at the beginning. We sure
could use some in the middle.

I understand about Daddy joining the church. It's mostly
to make Mommy feel better. Mommy's the real goods. There's
not a person on Sarvis Creek she hasn't done a good turn at
one time or another. Bernice loves her like a daughter would.

Funny thing, though—it's Mommy and Melissa who get along like a house on fire. Bernice and Charlene both a little jealous of my daughter Melissa. Little witch, with her computer talk and flirting with all the boys and a few grown men, too. I told Bernice to set her straight on things, but Bernice laughed and said, "I wish my head had been that straight when I was her age." Mommy seems to think so, too, but I don't think Mommy knows about the flirting part. Daddy does. When he told me about that time she happened upon Fergus and his crowd selling votes—and what in hell was Daddy doing there?—I thought I'd die. She was only twelve then. "You'd better start keeping an eye on her," he said, and I thought if Fergus touches a hair on her head, I'll kill him. I'm not the kind of man who kills people, so that scared me too, coming out with an old cliché like that. Bernice and me agreed she'd have to stop going into the hills alone. But Bernice said then what she says now: that Melissa knows where to draw the line. "You watch her," she said. "She generally knows who's safe and who isn't." I hope to God my wife is right. Especially now that my daughter has moved out of the magic circle and comes back to Kentucky full of stories that sound a little alien, a little strange to me.

For a long time, Bernice didn't look much older than Melissa does now, but she has developed a gray hair or two and a wrinkle or two, I guess. Her hair a sunny river that first time. Platinum blonde, they call it. Now she's had it cut short. Easier to take care of, she says, and I guess it is that. "Besides I'm an old woman now," she says, snuggling up to me in bed. I'm a lucky man where the women in my life are concerned. At least so far. Bernice wants to move to Ohio so bad she can taste it.

What to do about Daddy? Sitting up there on the platform not looking religious. They'll be praying over him soon enough, days of wailing and moaning. I'd like to be somewhere else. Mommy's going to need me. Charlene ain't up to it, it's plain. Something's been wrong there. Something more than her rotten marriage. Maybe it's that guy I saw her with. Or maybe it is her head. And Tessie's got her hands full at home. And somebody has to run the store and the post office. And Wal-Mart opened that store on Rocky Creek and it's taking away business. Good thing we've got Bernice's teaching money. Health insurance, too, through her. Tessie and Floyd don't have any.

I'll help campaign for Benjamin Tolliver if he wins the primary. Got to get some good men in. Men who'll see that we get our fair share. Ben's father was a Kennedy man. Best representative we ever had in Frankfort. Well, let's hope it's like father like son. Ben says right but will he do right? I didn't like the way he shined up to Curtis Midahl when Curtis joined us Friday evening. Curtis is slick and he's crooked and he's a big noise in bad places.

I sit here thinking about moving to Ohio. If we go, I know we won't come back. After Eddie called about the jobs at the GM plant, we got on the Internet and looked over things in Dayton. Bernice said, "And we could go to Cincinnati sometimes. Go to hear a symphony, maybe. Charlene and Bob went. Charlene said it was great." As for me, I'd like to go hear Dvorak's *New World Symphony* live, especially that part that sounds like "Going Home." Eddie said it'd be a while before GM got around to filling the jobs. I don't want to go. "Hell, Bernice," I said, "I'll take you up to Cincinnati. We don't have to move to Dayton for that."

I could go to night school, that's true. They got several colleges around there. But I could do that here if I tried hard. Bernice don't necessarily know what she's talking about, what it really would be like for us. She's visited here and there but she ain't never lived anywhere but here, unless you count when she went to college at Morehead.

I was working for the Sayhorn Mine, driving that coal truck when I met her. I had unloaded and was driving the truck back up along Calhoun Road, outside of town, thinking about my brand-new guitar, when I saw the two girls hitchhiking and one of them was beautiful, I thought, with that sunny head of hair, so I stopped. They were in no hurry to ride in a coal truck but I flirted with them a little and I pulled out my guitar and played a little bluegrass, Bill Monroe style. I'm lucky there, too. All I have to do with guitars or fiddles is play around with them for a while and then I can play just about anything I know the tune to. Even that old organ in Bernice's parents' home—I can play that, too.

The girls said they'd hitched down from Morehead. They were on their way home for spring break. The other girl lived over on Painter Fork, but Bernice lived right in town. Dr. Calhoun's daughter, she said with pride. (I'd never heard of the guy, but I pretended I had.) Well, I was game and said I'd take her right to her door. She looked at my truck and she broke down and giggled. "We'll take you up on that," she said. "Linda can call her brother from there, and he'll come pick her up."

Bernice's folks had a brick house with white shutters and I almost ran when I saw that living room. Two big couches and soft rugs and a pretty painting of a woman with a little girl on the wall (Renoir, Bernice said.) Her father wasn't there and her mother didn't seem too glad to see me, but she was real glad to see Bernice and she thanked me after she got through scolding Bernice for hitchhiking. I told her I agreed with her and we both looked at Bernice, who it was plain had no intention of changing her ways. "I told Daddy I needed a car," she said, "but he wouldn't listen." Her mother gave her that look, the "*We'll talk about this after he goes*" look. I was hanging around trying to figure out how I could see her again, but finally I had to go. Bernice has taught me what I know about Renoir. She says she disapproves of "reproductions" and she wishes her parents would replace that painting with somebody local. Somebody like Red Anson, I guess. He does us hillbillies in our hillbilly homes, almost like old-time photographs but sweeter and grimmer.

I was in the store the other day when Red came in wanting his pack of cigarettes. "Them things are going to kill you, Red," I said, because I've heard his coughing. He ignored me on that and he said, "Jeff, did ya ever hear of a man called St. John of the Cross?" I said I hadn't. He put a cigarette in his mouth and lit up. "I just wondered," he said. "My Sammy brought this book home the teacher lent him." I asked Bernice about it later and she said, "That's Charles, the new guy from up in Cleveland. Sammy Anson's too young for St. John of the Cross. Charles is lonely and he's trying to make friends out of his eighth-graders." I was relieved to hear her put the new teacher down. He's a good-looking man. He was out in front of the school talking to her one day when I went to pick her up, and I thought he was way too friendly with her, let alone with his eighth-graders. Bernice says he's smart. I've never cheated on Bernice. I'm not like my father.

***

That day the summer after I graduated from eighth grade, when I went with Daddy over to Rufus Branch. He had got to be friends with Mr. Tipton, who delivered pop for the Royal Crown Cola people, and for some reason Mr. Tipton hadn't shown up when he was supposed to and we were running low on pop. So Daddy took a notion to go pay him a visit and I begged to tag along. It was a hot day in July. The locusts were singing high in the dust and heat waves rose from the road. Daddy's old DeSoto seemed to stutter through them, I remember, and I felt the damp of my own sweat beneath me on the seat. The window was wide open and the car's hot wind tore against my bare arm, already red from hoeing corn.

Daddy has this habit of repeating things. For instance, he'll say, "It's going to come a big storm," and not a minute will go by and he'll say again, "A big storm," as though he's trying to convince you or maybe himself. When he does that, I always think of him as being alone and the words are fences around him. That day, it was a song. He was singing "I Am a Man of Constant Sorrow," and he sang it again and again. But not sadly. Kind of absentmindedly. Sitting beside him on the front seat, I felt lonely. I didn't play the guitar back then. I didn't know that Daddy's friend the coal miner who played on the local radio station was going to hand me his guitar in the fall and I would just play, just like that, like magic. I owe that guy, and I owe Daddy, who got me a guitar though we were low on money that winter.

The feel of the strings against your fingers, the sweet calluses. The music spilling out, running over.

It was a bad summer. Come fall, I had to go to the consolidated high school and Howie Jones, about twice my size, had promised to beat me up on the first day of school. Howie hated me because May Jane Bales kept giving me part of her lunch. And because I had smart-mouthed him a few times. Leave us not forget that. Poor Howie. Died drunk in a car wreck in his senior year. He never did beat me up, but Pete Arbiter did after I put a garter snake in his lunch box. Just for meanness. Because he was so stuck on himself. I think Howie was a little retarded. I should've been ashamed of myself.

Anyhow, I sat there beside Daddy, and when I wasn't worrying about Howie beating me up, I was dreaming about Oneida, who was built, and when I wasn't dreaming about Oneida, I was feeling the wind on my right arm and watching the green trees zip right on by as though they were in a hurry to join up with their brothers behind us.

We didn't talk. (Standing beside him when I was about five or so, and he'd let me help swing a case of pop down from Mr. Tipton's truck. I miss those old trucks with the open cases of pop stacked up high, glass flashing in the sunlight.) My daddy and me, we talk to make people like us but also to ward them off. Except me to Bernice, and in the quiet hours of the night Daddy to Mommy. I've heard them when they thought us kids were asleep. Or maybe they didn't care much. Maybe it just was the time when they were alone together. But there are things Daddy didn't tell Mommy. I wonder if the time will ever come when I don't tell things to Bernice. (I wonder if there are things that Bernice doesn't tell me.)

We turned off and left the river behind us and went up this one-way road alongside Rufus Branch, the car bumping and shaking in its dirt. Rufus Branch is a creek that mine pollution has got to in the last few years, but in my childhood it was deep and green in the shade of thick overhanging trees. Gone now.

All of a sudden, Daddy said, "You want to go swimming?" When I answered yes, as he knew I would, he reached down into the paper sack on the floor and pulled out our cutoffs. "Your mother hunted them up," he said. He parked on a wide spot off the road and said, "Here's about where your grandpa and us boys used to swim." Grandpa had died long ago, probably of the same kind of cancer that's getting Daddy now. Once Mommy told me she had seen Daddy crying at his father's funeral. Mommy tells a vivid story. I think that shook me more than Grandpa's distant death.

All the aunts and uncles gathering at the house after funerals. All that food and all those tears. I foundered on chicken and dumplings on the day Uncle Bryan was buried, did not touch them again for years.

My daddy Orson Caskill soon.

So on that very hot day, my daddy and me went behind some trees and put on our cutoffs and came out to horse around in the deep green water. A crawdad got my toe but not enough to do me any damage. Afterward, we dried off halfway on the thin old towel Mommy had put in the paper sack and, feeling cool, went on up Rufus Branch to Mr. Tipton's. He lived at the last of three houses not too far apart in a bit of bottomland along the creek. He had three boys and a girl, and they were all there, along with him and Mrs. Tipton, sitting on their big front porch drinking fresh-made lemonade. It turned out that Mr. Tipton had hurt his leg pulling up a stump in the garden and the doctor had told him to take a few days off. "But I'll be around your way by next week," he told Daddy anxiously. And Daddy said for him not to worry about it, everything would be jake, and he patted Mr. Tipton on the shoulder and smiled at Mrs. Tipton and asked if they had any lemonade to spare. Mrs. Tipton rushed in the house to get it and I rushed down the steps with the other children. They had some worms in a tomato can of dirt and we went fishing. Daddy had settled himself in a chair beside Mr. Tipton and they fell to talking politics, I know, because they always did, and shook their heads over what the politicians were doing to the country. So I figured I had a while.

It must have been an hour later, after a few bugs bit me and the sweat ran down my face and the fish weren't biting, at least not for me, that I made my way back up the bank and to the Tiptons' front porch. Mr. Tipton was still sitting there, all by himself. He looked worried when he saw me. "Come up and have a seat, son," he said. "Your daddy'll be back soon."

But I felt ill at ease. It was one thing fishing with his kids, but I'd never been alone with Mr. Tipton. "Where'd he go?" I blurted out.

Tipton jerked his head toward the other houses. "Just visiting," he said. "He said to tell you to wait on him here."

"All right," I told him, but I was curious. Curiosity killed the cat. I made like I was heading back for the creek. But instead I went along the backs of the two other houses. It was so hot everybody had their windows open and I figured I wouldn't have much trouble finding him. And I didn't. I heard his voice at the far house and then I heard a woman's voice and, instead of knocking at the back door, I thought it would be fun to stick my head in the window and say hello. So I looked through the window, and there was my Daddy, Orson, with his arms around a red-haired woman. They were both laughing. I sneaked away and went over to the creek bank and sat by myself for a good long while. By the time I made myself go back to the Tiptons', everybody else was sitting on the front porch again, including Daddy. "Where you been?" Daddy asked, giving me a funny look. "Wading in the creek," I said and held up my wet pants leg. "No wonder we didn't ketch any fish," Tipton's oldest boy said, laughing. They all laughed, and then Daddy and me got back in the truck. We didn't say a word on the way home, and I remember that I felt sick and I didn't know what to say when I saw Mommy. I would never do that to Bernice. At least I don't think I would. I've often wondered if Daddy repeated himself on this over the years. Not recently at any rate. I've been working alongside him for twenty years now and I think I'd know.

The other thing in his life that he keeps to himself is Fergus. Even now, after him joining the church, they pal around together from time to time. When Fergus turns up, him and Daddy go off drinking or hunting or fishing or whatever else they get up to. I've had no time for Fergus from the time Tessie told me that he bothered Charlene. I would've told Daddy but Tessie said no, she promised Char. Char was afraid he'd hurt Daddy. When we were little, Mommy would gather us up out of Fergus's way anytime he came to the house. No kind words from Fergus, just pats on the head and maybe a joke. Once he happened to step on my foot and when I cried out, he laughed and said, "Orson, you got to toughen this young'un up." Most men, they've got some good in them. I used to know a man who raped and murdered his wife, but he seemed to make a pretty decent life when he got out of the pen. Not Fergus. He's what Melissa calls "awesome," but in the bad sense. I take my family home whenever Fergus shows up. Sometimes I'm lonesome for a man friend, though, maybe even someone like Ted Dalday the former killer.

***

Where I knew Ted was up in Indiana. He was from our neck of the woods, but after he got out of prison, he found a job at an air-conditioning factory in Ardahoe, outside Indianapolis. My second cousin Eddie worked there, too, before he got the job at GM in Dayton. (Eddie and I have always been buddies, though his mother fell out with Daddy over Fergus, who, she said, sold dope to her oldest son. Eddie's big brother got doped up and ran away from home, all the way to California. He sent one postcard and nobody's heard from him since.)

It was after the time when I met Bernice, but I hadn't figured out how to get a date with her, knowing just from being in their house and meeting her mother that her parents wouldn't like the idea. And I was sick of driving that god-damned coal truck and I was feeling like adventure. I didn't have a car, so I hitchhiked all the way to Ardahoe, and that's a story in itself. But I got there all right, and Eddie introduced me to the foreman and he gave me a job. Eddie had him a one-bedroom apartment on a leafy street and he put me up 'til I could afford a place of my own. I didn't care much for the work, though, not from the beginning. It was an assembly line. "What's to like?" Eddie asked. (He's always picking up ways of talking from people he hangs around with.) "You do the work and then you're out of there." I figured he was right and any-how I was planning to rise in the world and get beyond the assembly line pretty quick.

I took a small room in someone's house close to the plant. Well, I had to live close because I didn't have a car. (Even if I'd lived on Eddie's street, we worked different shifts and I couldn't ride to work with him.) It was like an oven in that room. Pulling down the shade didn't do no more than take the glare off the heat. And at night the only light was a light bulb dangling from the ceiling. The woman that rented it out was a widow living on a small pension and she'd given up hope long ago. Her gray hair was always mussed and her clothes were always a little dirty. So was the house. But I figured I'd save up and buy me a car and then, as Eddie would say, I'd be out of there. At least she didn't mind my guitar playing. Playing at night in the still heat and the moon rising and dreaming of Bernice. Blue moon of Kentucky keep on shining.

And it was fun hanging around with Eddie, drinking too much but not enough for serious trouble. One weekend we went to Chicago. Eddie knew somebody there who used to work at the plant and would be glad to put us up for the night (in return for Eddie's company). So off we went. You got to figure that at this point I hadn't even been in Lexington proper, and Chicago blew my mind (as Melissa would say). It wasn't just that it was big, though it was plenty that. It was also tall when you got downtown. We went along that big blue lake. I got an ambition to live in one of the tall buildings by the lake. Eddie laughed. "You'd better get to be foreman fast," he said.

But the minute I told him that, I thought about the hills and the dark, cool inside of my daddy's store and my mother's broad, gentle face. I looked over at Eddie, who had the long, lean face of the Caskills, and asked, "D'ye ever think of going home?"

"When I retire," he said. "I'm going to buy me a little place on Painter Fork, you know there where that high ridge above the river dips down to the creek. Covered with pine trees." It was pretty there, and close to his sisters and brothers.

When we got back to Ardahoe, he heard that he got the job in Dayton. So pretty soon I was alone at Ardahoe, working a job that was beginning to drive me crazy and coming home to that suffocating room. Winter had come, but it was still suffocating, because she kept the heat turned up so high. "I freeze easy," she said when I complained.

Rob Danvers, a work buddy, asked me if I wanted to go to the high school's basketball game on a Saturday night. Well, I always liked basketball. I played passing guard for two years, and I was pretty good at it. Used to practice five or six days a week. Me and Eddie. Eddie was taller, though, and he played center.

When Rob picked me up on Saturday, there were two other guys in the car. Jack Somebody-or-other and Bill, or was it Burt?, and Ted Dalday. Bill and Jack were men in their late twenties like Rob. (I was younger, about twenty then.) Bill and Jack were both married, and Jack had some children. They all worked at the plant. Ted Dalday was a foreman, Rob warned me, twinkling an eye at the older man. As the new guy, I sat in the back with Bill and Jack, me in the middle. Or maybe Ted got the front seat because he was older. They were drinking beer and talking about Ardahoe's chances of playing in the state tournament that was coming up. Nobody talked about work. Rob and Jack were Ardahoe-born, and Bill was from Michigan City. Ted hesitated a minute, then said he was from Knott County. Well, anybody could have told he was an East Kentuckian just by listening to him talk.

"How long you been up here?" I asked.

He hesitated again and said about five years. Then somebody changed the subject. It was probably Rob. I learned that Ted's son was on the basketball team. "Annie's bringing Carol Sue to the game," Ted said. "They're letting me have a night out with the boys." They were all in the habit of getting together once a month or so. If it wasn't a ball game, it was the pool hall on West Main, and if it wasn't the pool hall, it was some bar.

They began to invite me along and I was mighty glad of the company. We didn't talk too much about ourselves or our kin the way men won't, but I got to know a fair amount about them all the same. Rob finally filled me in about Ted. "He had a beautiful wife, to hear him tell it anyway and if you see his daughter you'll believe it, and he went crazy when she started stepping out on him. One night she come home about three, after leaving the kids at her mother's and Ted spending half the night looking for everybody before he thought to go to her mother's. He left the kids there and went back home. She come in around three and he went crazy. Raped her and strangled her. The judge said there were extenuating circumstances because of her behavior, and Ted got off with ten years. They made him serve eight of them." Part of it was, Rob told me, Ted'd been out of work for a year and she was stepping out with some hotshot from the mine where he had worked.

"Why didn't he go after the hotshot?" I asked.

"Didn't have a chance to, I guess. She was screaming and things were falling. Somebody heard the ruckus and called the sheriff's office. Then after he was released, the mother let him have the children back without a fight. Said she'd spent enough time on his brats, which gives you some idea of what kind of family he married into. The kids were glad to be out of there, he says. She worked them half to death and kept them out of school whenever she took a notion. Ted got his unmarried cousin Annie to come north with him and look after Carol Sue. Somebody at the prison helped him get a job at the plant, and he worked so hard they made him foreman in two years. That, and all the men like him. But he has trouble with the boy."

I'd heard enough, so I didn't ask what kind of trouble.

It was about a month later that Ted showed up at my door one evening. "Would you come over to my house?" he asked right off. "I hate to ask you, but I can't think of anybody else I'd trust. Rob's girlfriend is in town, and I don't want to ask Bill or Jack."

"What's this all about, Ted?" I asked him.

"Annie's mother's real sick, in the hospital, and they have to operate. She needs to get down there, so I'm taking her and Carol Sue, but my boy won't go and I can't leave him alone. Untelling what he'd get up to."

The boy was practically grown. Sixteen or seventeen. "I don't know that I'd be any big help," I told him.

"I'll just be gone tomorrow and part of the next day," he said. "Just for two nights." There was much trouble in his eye, so I shrugged my shoulders and threw some clothes into a paper sack and went with him.

They had a gray frame house about ten blocks from where I lived. It was a leafy street like Eddie's had been, and the house was freshly painted. There was a sagging glider on the porch, but the porch was clean and neat. Annie let us in. She was a timid-looking woman with a nice smile. The girl beside her had probably inherited her mother's looks. She had shiny black hair and big blue eyes. They both looked scared and, seeing the boy, who was standing back in the inner doorway, I could see why. He was madder than a hornet. It was clear that the person he was maddest at was Ted. Ted introduced me directly to him and asked him to shake hands with me. The boy refused, which was fine with me. I'm not much on hand-shaking and I could see how Ted's pushing him like that didn't help any. As they glared at each other, I was reminded of the time I tried to keep Spot and Bandit, our two dogs at home when I was a child, from jumping a groundhog. Tessie had found him in the woods with a broken leg and she was making a pet of him. But Spot and Bandit weren't having it. They barked and threatened and I tried sassing them and prodding them but they paid no attention to me. They did what they were born to do.

The son disappeared into the back part of the house. Ted went after him and I heard them shouting at each other. Annie and the girl eyed each other uneasily and Annie asked me if I wanted a cup of coffee. I said yes just to give them something to do and myself a breathing space.

Then I heard a door slam and it went silent at the back. Ted came back with a suitcase and apologized for his son's behavior. "Maybe I did wrong to bring you over," he said. "Allen's gone now and I don't know where. Got so I never know where."

I figured I had a pretty good idea. I'd seen a place three blocks from the plant where teenagers got together in the evenings and made a rough noise. However, I didn't figure it'd do any good to go looking for the boy. I let Ted show me around and then him and the women left and I settled myself down in front of the TV. I didn't have a TV in my own room and I didn't like to watch it with the widow, so this was fun. Ted had told me to help myself in the kitchen, so I got a box of Cheez-Its and a Coke and settled back. I thought I'd wait up for the boy anyhow.

It was almost two o'clock when he came home. I could smell the alcohol a mile off. He just looked at me, answered my hello, shrugged, and went along to his room. I went to Ted's room and got ready for bed. My shift started at 6 a.m. I wasn't worried about it, though. At that age, I didn't think much about doing without a good night's sleep. Well, I certainly didn't get one. In a little while he knocked on my door. I opened it and he stood there, sizing me up. "You ain't that much older than me," he said.

"No. I guess I ain't."

"But he trusts you to do right," he said. "Not me. His own son, and he don't trust me an inch."

"He's just worried for you," I said. "Me, I don't matter so much to him."

"You matter enough for him to haul you over here to lord it over me."

"Do I look like lording it?" I asked.

"Why don't you go on home?"

"I promised him I'd stay."

"Promises to killers don't count."

I was shocked. "You shouldn't talk about your dad that way. He strikes me as being a pretty decent guy."

"What do you know about it? You're like him, sitting in front of that television every night. Ordering me around. Tells everybody about how I play ball, oh, yeah, that's the one thing

I do he likes. He can show off to people, like he does with Carol's good looks."

"He's probably tired evenings," I answered feebly.

"He just don't care. I'm going to leave here the minute I graduate."

"Give him a chance," I said, knowing it was a silly thing, a weak thing to say.

"Like he gave my mother a chance?"

"Well, Allen, even if you were right, it don't do no good for you to throw your own life away."

"Oh, I got plans," he said, and the way he said it made me cold. But I found myself liking this screwed-up teenager as he stood there in his stocking feet sassing the world but with a hopeful look in his brown eyes. He looked a lot like his daddy.

He was still in bed the next morning when I left for work at 5:30. I knew he had a ball game that evening, so I figured I'd go to that. I enjoyed the ball games anyhow, and I thought Ted would be happy that I went. I didn't think his son would be, though. He made like he didn't see me there, all right, and he didn't get home until after midnight. I came out of Ted's room, where I was reading a Zane Gray western I'd found on the dresser, and said, "Good game. You played good," and he had. He gave me an evil look and went to his room without speaking. It was a good-sized house, a bedroom for each one.

I fell asleep but not for long. He woke me up with a gun in his hand and said, "Give me what money you got."

"You sure you want to do this?"

"Just gimme the money and you won't get hurt," he said like somebody in a bad western. He looked awful young standing there with that big heavy .45 in his hand.

I figured I could take him and that was my mistake. The bullet made a nasty gash in my shoulder and I started bleeding like a stuck pig. (I've helped kill a few hogs in my time, so I'd say that description is just right.) He didn't try to kill me. He could have. I sat down on the edge of the bed and dragged my wallet out of my jeans pocket. A twenty and some singles. That's all he got. He disappeared then, and I managed to drive myself to the hospital and of course they reported it to the police anyway and Ted came home to an awful mess.

"Couldn't you handle him no better than that?" Ted asked sadly.

I eyed him.

"I can't handle him myself," he said, shrugging his shoulders. "He don't really remember his mother, but their grandma made sure they got filled in on the details. I'm sure Rob's told you all about that. Rob's good-hearted but he's got a big mouth. Allen ain't never forgiven me. Maybe if their grandmother had treated them different. Maybe if I wasn't so messed up myself. I'm sorry about your shoulder."

After they cleaned and bandaged my shoulder at the hospital, I had gone back to Ted's so I could fill him in, so now he drove me home. "And what am I going to do with Carol? You saw her. Men'll be after her. It'll be her mother all over again." I hoped he didn't find the same remedy if that was the case. I didn't think he would, that he was now the gentle, caring man that had become my friend.

They found the boy two days later, sleeping up some back alley in Bloomington. They released him in Ted's care. And I guess things went on as before. All I knew was I didn't want to spend my life in Ardahoe. I thought of being back in the Caskill store, standing behind the counter and putting the cans on the shelves, just so, and people coming in to get what they needed and see what mail they got and saying howdy, how're you today, it's right hot out there, ain't it? I thought about the girl with the hair like sunlight. I thought about walking into the house and Mommy fixing me fried chicken with gravy and some of that downhome cornbread for which she knows just how much buttermilk to use and sitting down to supper with them all there. I packed up my cardboard suitcase and went home. And I mean to stay home, but then there's Bernice and all her daydreams.

When you play the guitar good, your head is in your fingers, your heart is in your fingers. I went home and Mommy fried the chicken (after I killed it for her) and Daddy said he'd sure be glad to have me back in the store. I went home and played my heart out sitting on the back porch. Then I went to find Bernice. I love my wife, but we're not moving to Dayton. That's my Sunday thought, I guess.

11. 2004: MELISSA'S POSTLUDE

—

With my shoulders resting against pillow that in turn rests against wall, I am writing on my yellow legal pad about Adam and Eve. The tree of knowledge sprang from the seed of nostalgia when God cast them out of the garden. Life, which had been part of them, became an object, to be desired, to be explored in all its labyrinthine lineaments. The garden could be fancied to have been the bright limbs of our original parents. Cast out of our childhoods, most of us retain the enchanted circle that time transcribes in our memory. Housman's lines. Those blue, remembered hills, those happy highways forever lost. When they were cast out, Adam and Eve, and their progeny, begat the world so that they might recreate Eden.

It is night and the light on my bedside table creates a nest where my bent head nods to the legal pad like a hungry bird. Outside, in the Chicago night, it is early August and the temperature is about ninety-five degrees. The white dome of the Museum of Science and Industry floats suspended in the greater darkness. Beyond the museum is the moonstruck field of the lake, the city's great enemy. As the million noises of the

139

place create its mayhem, chunks of the day, the month, the years are made powerless, rendered into music by the endless soughing, real and imagined, of the lake. All the city's images are subsumed by this great metaphor. We stare at it out of bus windows, train windows, car windows, and the city is erased.

I kept a lake journal for a year and registered forty-two colors. Pale violet morning lake. Deep blue midsummer lake. Dirty gray December lake. Stormy lake green with white-caps. Whistler lakes, Winslow Homer lakes, Monet lakes, the wine-dark lake. Here in the city, the lake is my Kentucky. The branches on lakeside trees gesticulate toward God, shout-ing Appalachian hosannas. (Because I am a self-confessed Appalachian and a Kentuckian, simplistic conclusions about me are possible when I say such words as "God.")

Then again, the lake is the city's memorial. We pluck memories from it as we go by but they sink back into the deep slime of the lake bed. Sometimes I have glimpsed their contours as the plane passed over on its way to Ohio, to New York, even to Paris. (But never directly to Kentucky. Until a year ago, I had gone to my home state only as a child goes, in the company of my parents.)

Do not mistake me. I carry inside me that great meta-phor Kentucky, and I develop a mental stutter when I talk to my Chicago acquaintances about my life. Unlike my younger brother and sister, who were born in Ohio, I am a bona fide Kentuckian. Unlike my mother, who denies her Kentuckyness, I choose to remember the Kentucky of my childhood very well. This I share with my father, Jeff, who never wanted to leave.

Like my mother, though, I have wanted to be free to grasp this brave new world: on the one hand, a Hollywood devo-tee, or, more literarily, an Emma Bovary seeking bright, noisy rooms. On the other, a serious pursuer of the larger life, the room of one's own. So here in Hyde Park, in the vicinity of the University of Chicago, where the lofty and the passionate mostly manage to trump intellectual pretentiousness, here I have, if not yet a room of my own, a room in which I am most certainly alone.

Today I have received a letter from my mother, Bernice— whom I call Mommy more often than not, as I call my father Daddy. Let's say it's a Kentucky thing. Like a Russian diminutive. Brothers and sisters either get their names lengthened, so that Ann becomes Annie (we love the "-ie" endings) or shortened, so that Thomas Jefferson becomes T.J. These rules apply also to longtime neighbors, husbands and wives, close friends and lovers.

Mommy writes that Fergus has not only got religion; he has gone Catholic. There aren't many Catholics in eastern Kentucky, but I can see where Fergus would feel the need of a stronger religion, begging the Baptists' pardon. It would need to be a strong religion indeed to envelop Fergus and come out unscathed.

Mommy continues, "*Whatever priest confessed him probably had to wash out his ears with lye soap.*" I laugh over that. My mother grows on me as I get older.

My father can't stand Fergus either. Fergus is one of the mysteries of my past. But his friend Orson, my grandfather, is the greater mystery. When we lived in Kentucky and were visiting Grandpa and Grandma's and Fergus came by, Daddy would soon whisper in Mommy's ear and she would find me and off the three of us would go. Grandma Sarah Beth always looked as though she'd like to join us, but instead she would just retreat to the kitchen. In my early years I didn't understand their revulsion. Fergus was a beautiful man then. The light shone in his curly blond-brown hair, and his eyes were a bright, shallow blue fringed with thick lashes. And in hindsight—in both meanings—he was built like a Greek god. He would look at me and invite me to laugh with him as he told my grandfather about doings at the county courthouse. Fergus liked to observe trials. Risk-taking of a kind, I suppose.

"Yeah," my father would grumble to my mother. "If there was any justice in the world, he'd've been the object of several trials by now."

"Shhh," Mommy would say, looking back at me.

Jennifer, who also has been working on a dissertation but is up for her defense and ready to move on, tells me she envies me my parents, who not only write letters but come to see me from time to time. When I complained about Mommy's eagerness to be fully bourgeois (her father *is* a doctor, but she dreams of the full-fledged mainstream crème de la crème sense) and about Daddy's half-life since we left Kentucky, she reciprocated by filling me in on her Cinderella story. Her father, a famous neurosurgeon, divorced her Park Avenue mother. He got custody because her mother wanted it that way. Her mother moved to London, and her father remarried. "They sent me off to school right away."

Jennifer and Cheu and I get together occasionally and go to evening lectures, preferably to the ones where food is served. Jennifer is a tall, thin redhead dressed in jeans and Parisian shirts. Cheu is short and thin and firmly Korean. I am slightly zoftig and have large brown eyes that hide my critical faculties. One evening last January, we went to hear a Harvard professor lecture on Thucydides and the twenty-first century. (One of my professors told me that fifteen years ago this speaker had given approximately the same lecture, then entitled "Thucydides and the Twentieth Century.") The lecture was held in an auditorium/lounge punctuated by plump armchairs, which had been moved to the periphery to make room for the folding chairs on which we sat. The lecturer was Greek (and very good, I thought, even if it was a repeat performance), and the member of the classics department who introduced him was an Englishman with what the novels call a "plummy" accent. "Stephen says he's a former lover of Irene Pappas," Jennifer hissed. Stephen, her boyfriend and a fledgling journalist, likes to invent gossip. It doesn't do to repeat his stories as gospel truth, I have to my embarrassment discovered.

After the lecture, on our wintry way over to the reception, Cheu said, "Thucydides and Machiavelli belong to the same flock [his variation on birds of a feather]. The West should have listened to Buddha." Cheu's family lived in India for a few years and converted to Buddhism while there. He shook his head now. Cheu takes his learning seriously. So do I, but with a grain of salt. I am reminded of the character Justine in Lawrence Durrell's *Alexandrian Quartet*. The moment when she discovers that she will not find the ultimate truth in the books she devours she changes her whole life, though not necessarily for the better.

The reception was hosted by Dr. Darcy Brant (better known to me as Darcy Anne Titwell), my dissertation adviser. She is a rare bird, a native of Sarvis, Kentucky, who has made the academic big time. Once upon a time, I think, she and Grandpa Orson were lovers. Now she has written the Caskill family history. (She has in the past kept me at a distance, but it's hard for her to do that now.)

Cheu was a little morose that January evening. His pretty Indian girlfriend had thrown him over for a weak-chinned Wasp who was getting his MBA. Watching Cheu watch the crowd, I thought of Sherman, who belonged to one of the university's multidisciplinary "committees," populated by the oddballs whose ambitions or tastes cannot be contained in a single discipline. Sherman was from New Orleans. His mother's family owned a good part of the French Quarter. His father ran two of his mother's restaurants. Sherman was predictably crazy about Dixieland jazz and Muddy Waters. I was crazy about Sherman. We had met at one of Dr. Brant's parties, when he came to my corner to check out this marginal being. It didn't bother Sherman that I wasn't a member of the in-crowd. As far as Sherman was concerned, he and his friends automatically constituted an in-crowd.

He had come to the university primarily to satisfy his curiosity and secondarily to write a book on Baudelaire (it's out now; I saw it in the window of 57th Street Books the other day). He would entertain lavishly in his newly acquired condo, to which both faculty members and students flocked. Sherman wasn't particularly witty. Partly, of course, it was his wealth. I told him so toward the end, and he turned his hand over in the way he had as though he were plucking up a statement, a complaint, an idea, and then dismissing it. "That's how it is," he said, almost sternly.

The way Sherman listened was a kind of genius, though. Sometimes in the middle of something else—a lecture, perhaps, or an argument about politics that he was having with another person altogether—he would turn to you and refer to a detail that named you, some detail peripheral to whatever you had been telling him but all the more telling for its being thrown off like that. His friendship and his lovemaking had been utterly direct and then after a while he was gone. Jennifer's Stephen had warned me about that. "It's wonderful while he's there but suddenly he isn't. He does it to friends. He does it to lovers." But I didn't trust Stephen's judgment because I knew that he himself was restless. He would go away, and Jennifer would take him back. "You're my queen," he would tell her. "The others are entertainments."

Sherman took me seriously, me and my history. "Perhaps you *should* go back for a year or two," he said.

"Do you have any idea how difficult that might be?" I asked him.

"Yes, and how easy it would be," he replied. "You could stay with your father's mother, with Sarah Beth."

"Why her?" I asked just to hear what he would say. Because of course I could but I didn't think I had told him so.

"Remember that story you told me about your aunt's breakdown? You said, 'If she had trusted Grandma, she might have been all right.' There's always comfort in your voice when you speak of her."

Oh, yes, I was crazy about Sherman. And then he wasn't

there anymore. I would see him at lectures with an older woman who had exotic eyebrows and what I interpreted as a patrician bearing. Devastated, I almost lost my fellowship. Jennifer listened patiently and handed me tissues. She and Stephen took me downtown to various events. After about two months of this, my pride returned and I got back to work, just in time. By then Sherman had left for New York. "Feel sorry for him," Jennifer said. And after a while I saw that she might be right, but the moment I was alone and lifted my head from my work, emptiness threatened to immure me. I needed to go home. I called my parents and asked them how they would feel about going down to Osier County when the quarter was over.

That January evening after the lecture on Thucydides, Dr. Brant's reception was in full swing. The guest of honor had entered and made his way to her, attended by the classics professor who had introduced him. I was near enough to hear the visitor and Dr. Brant reminisce about a Parisian night spot with which they were both familiar. Heady stuff. Cheu offered to walk me home. I too didn't want to stay and I accepted. On the way, we were initially silent. My thoughts were circling about a phone call from my mother. I wondered if Cheu was thinking about Korea, but suddenly he was telling me a tale about Chicago.

He had gone to the Pilsen neighborhood with a woman friend to see the Frida Kahlo exhibit and to eat Mexican food afterward. Wandering around after the exhibit, they had been late entering the restaurant, and by the time they exited it was almost dark and a fair distance from the bus stop. A group of teenagers had surrounded them. "Did they have guns?" I asked. "I don't know. But they had knives. They showed them to us. They made jokes about Claire." I had met Claire, who wore skimpy sweaters and high-heeled boots. She was also a serious student of the Chinese language—and forthright. "Claire told them to get lost. I didn't know what to say. I was petrified, as you say it—I don't know whether for her or for myself. I thought Claire was making matters worse. One boy said something about her breasts, and Claire said, 'I can tell you, honey, these aren't silicon.' And he laughed, and then they went away."

"What did Claire say?"

"I asked her, 'How did you know to say that?' 'I've got a kid brother,' she said. But something bad could have happened, Melissa. Chicago is a dangerous place."

This morning, I walked down 55th Street on the other side of the train tracks. This stretch of street always looks a little grimy and grumpy. Perhaps it's remembering the old days, before the university cleaned up the neighborhood in a regrettably pedestrian way, ridding 55th Street, I'm told, of a string of bars. As I emerged from the leafy canopy of southern Hyde Park, 55th Street looked bare and open to adverse persuasion. A train roared overhead. The businesses looked drab and tentative. People who had not had fortunate lives lingered on the sidewalks. Thinking about nervous things, I stood there and let the bus get away. It felt like an affront. I could so easily have crossed the empty street against the light. But 55th Street counsels caution, though its menace at that moment was not really a physical one.

This Chicago neighborhood, Hyde Park, is pretty well gentrified now, but it is surrounded by ghettoes. An older friend of mine tells about the week Martin Luther King, Jr., was murdered, and there were snipers in the neighborhood. The university's students must have been shaken up. That kind of unease still exists here around the edges, so to speak, attended by guilt. The Have-Nots are too close for comfort and some of them will keep reminding us of their existence. It may just be a too-thin young man in a too-thin coat on a zero day selling a newspaper put out by the homeless. Or it may be a threat of snatched purses and once in a while what we call crimes against the person. All of a sudden on a leafy street you find yourself alone with someone who probably doesn't live in the neighborhood and your tension level goes up, though the person may have perfectly blameless reasons for being there. And in Hyde Park, the felt division between the Have and the Have-Nots is largely one of color, though there are many middle-class Blacks in the area.

I had known only what might be called the leafy side of eastern Kentucky. My father told me that in Grandma Sarah Beth's day what he fancifully called the leafiness had won out more often than not, but continued unemployment and increasing drug use, along with the decimations perpetrated by the coal companies, had changed the landscape. Everything else was rumor.

I had liked to go climbing on Sarvis Mountain. One day in my twelfth year, being late, I made my way down a steep descent to the road that led from the schoolhouse to my mother's friend Alice's house, where I was expected. It was pretty steep all right, but I was a hill child, used to vertical locomotion. With sensuous pleasure I felt the rich dirt and the newly rustling leaves slide beneath my feet and I put my hand out to tough-barked trees to catch my downward flight. After that, the going was flatter, and I came upon the old Brassart flat, where a family by that name had lived long ago. I saw that it still got a good deal of foot use and the occasional car or truck, but there were no houses in sight.

Anyhow, being late, I stepped smartly along, beginning to hurry as I thought of my mother's anger. I heard voices in front of me, men's voices. There was some sort of clearing ahead. Had I been canny, had I listened to dark rumors, I would have hurried directly off the flat and quietly continued downhill at a steeper slant. But I was twelve, well-loved and well-cared-for. As I emerged into the clearing, I saw to my left a group of men and two or three women in bright clothing, like flowers on a dusty bush. Two men were lying on the grass, though the ground must have been cold. It was October after all and even the heat at midday carried a fledgling chill. The people were noisy. Several of them were drinking something (the women, too) and I was not so sheltered that I didn't recognize a drunk when I saw one. Once in a while even, my father would sit quietly at the kitchen table with a bottle of whisky when he thought I had retired to my room and I would hear him say maudlin things in a shaky voice. My mother would send me off to bed and she, too, would retire and leave him talking to himself in the kitchen. Other men under the influence had not seemed so tractable when they showed up somewhere on the road or in Grandpa's store.

I knew this was no place for me, but by this time I was halfway past and I thought I could glide on by and continue downhill. But Big John Colby, an out-of-work miner whose boy was in my class at school, saw me and shouted, "Well, looky here" as he moved in my direction. Several heads turned and I didn't know how to be polite without stopping in my tracks. So I froze and he came over to me, followed by three other men whom I did not know. Big John didn't seem to recognize me. He grabbed me by the arm and said, "C'mon over and join us, girl." I knew enough, too, about the looks in men's eyes to know I was conceivably in trouble. I tried to break away, but his clutch grew tighter and suddenly they were around me in a circle. "Let her go, John," someone behind me said, and, half-turning, I saw Fergus. But the look in his eyes was the worst look of all. "We'll just invite her over to the shack," he said, laughing. The shack was a three-sided affair on the far side of the clearing. As they herded me inside, I saw tables with gallon jugs on them. I had seen corn liquor before. Grandpa Orson was a friend of the sheriff, and once in a while the sheriff gave him a small jar of confiscated moonshine. He would give me a teaspoonful and I would make a face. That was what I was supposed to do.

There was also a cracked bowl with tiny cigarettes in it. Someone near me was smoking one and there was a sweet smell in the air. And there were a few stacks of money on the front table, behind which two men sat as though they had business there. I wondered if some kind of gambling was going on. There was a partition in the back of the shack, a hidden place.

Then there was my third cousin Dick, who lived way over on Juniper Creek, looking at me and saying, "How come Melissa is here?" adding weakly, "That's Orson's granddaughter, Fergus."

"Just tend to your own business," Fergus said.

Dick averted his eyes and shambled away. I saw someone get up from a rickety chair and make his shadowy way toward the front. A tall, thin figure with newly stooping shoulders and the magnificent head of silver hair that chemotherapy had not touched. It was my grandfather. He didn't look at me but at Fergus. "Thank you for bringing my granddaughter over," he said. "I was just getting ready to leave and I can give her a ride home."

Fergus didn't say anything and we walked away. It didn't really occur to me to wonder what Grandpa Orson was doing there. He came over and took my hand. "Time to be goin'," he said, wonderfully present. I felt the force of the man behind the thin, whimsical face that he always turned toward his family.

"Thank you, Grandpa," I said awkwardly.

Looking sideways at me, he said, "They wouldn't have hurt you. I bet your daddy don't know you're running all over the hills by yourself."

"What were they doing, Grandpa?"

He was silent for a long moment, then said, "Well, it was gambling but in a way it was selling votes. Don't you tell nobody you know that." I never did. I loved it that he told me.

When we got to the place where I should have met my mother an hour ago, I thought Grandpa would come with me into Alice's house. But he didn't budge from behind the wheel.

As I got out, Mommy standing on Alice's porch with arms akimbo, he said, "Be good now," and he reached over and patted my shoulder as I climbed down from the cab. I stood there hangdog and took the scolding that I so deserved. Later on, Grandpa said something to Daddy, I don't know how much, and Daddy told Mommy and they forbade me to roam the hills by myself. I never forgave Fergus. He took my hills away from me.

From that day, Grandpa Orson treated me like a grownup. I missed the easy whimsicality he meted out to the young. There were, also, no longer those outings with my father. "Stay with your mother," he'd say when he left for one of his fishing adventures. Mommy was daydreaming about Ohio and, beyond that, some bright urban world.

I sit here, propped up by pillows, in a still pool of light surrounded by the Chicago night and dream about a small patch of map somewhere east and south of the Bluegrass. My grandparents, my father's parents, Orson and Sarah Beth, are for me its Edenic essence, its once upon a time, its Ur-people. (Grandpa Orson remains so, though he is dead.) Theirs is the myth that sustains us who have fallen out of grace into other places, into history. Yet Orson was the first to leave, on his way to war. He sat up there dying on the platform on that Ur day, a Sunday after my twelfth birthday, when Emile and Bertha got married in that church formed by Sarah Beth's family, while the rest of us looked at him and, because we could not bear the sight, at ourselves sitting in that large, plain room that held that day so many Caskills and Alsecks and Wrights and Titwells.

Last August when I heard from Osier College, I called Grandma Sarah Beth in the morning, even before I called my parents, and told her that I had decided to return to Kentucky, to accept an invitation so long in coming after my application. ("You must try for it," Jennifer said. "You'd never forgive yourself if you didn't," and Cheu nodded agreement.) Classes started in three weeks. They had answered so late in the year that it seemed impromptu. Osier is a poor school; they probably weren't sure up until a week before that they would be able to fill the position. My own decision was provisional, tentative. There was a one-year contract, renewable from year to year, so that I could always escape and return to Hyde Park if I found it impossible, if I discovered that you can't go home again.

***

So last winter I sat again in the new church, as my family still called it, though it was built when Aunt Charlene was a girl. The wood church that my great-great-grandfather built was little more than a ruin now. We stopped using it entirely when an extra room was added to the new church in the year 2000. It was very old, as Grandma says regretfully whenever she sees the ruin, which is practically every Sunday. She herself is bent with time these days.

As a nonmember, on those rare occasions when I have attended, I do not find myself on the bare wooden platform, where the "saved" women still sit on one side of the preachers, the men on the other, in this religion that I rejected long ago but which echoes in my veins. My ancestors' pictures still hang on the wall back of the platform. My great-grandfather's picture had recently been added. He wore a black suit with a watch chain across the vest, the way I remembered seeing him outside the car looking in and talking to Grandpa Orson. He was, as they say, great old at the time. His daughter Sarah Beth says that he always dressed in the same black suit every Sunday and she cannot remember when he bought the previous one. They buried him in the last one. Great-Grandma, standing uncomfortably beside him in her long print dress, her hair braided around her head, died before I was born.

Like Grandpa Orson, I prefer Sunday afternoons to these

churchly mornings: given time, found time, when a few hours stretch out eternally, perhaps in summer on my parents' back porch in Ohio, in the lounge chair with its footrest and faded cushions, watching sunlight and shadows mystify the lawn and the yellow string of goldfinches feeding on the net bag that holds the seeds peculiar to finches and the humming-birds whirring at their own feeding station and the occasional squirrel running across the lawn to some improbable destination.

I was sitting last winter in the new church because I had left my room in Hyde Park to take the teaching job at the small college in Osier County. Looking in the *Chronicle of Higher Education* for a job anywhere, I had seen Osier College's ad for a teacher of freshman composition and sophomore literature. Forgetting any other possible job openings, I had urgently sent my brief curriculum vitae and the cover letter proclaiming my native status, my eagerness to return home, not knowing whether they would even respond and, if they did, whether I really wanted to go. Jennifer said, "You have to try. You'll never be satisfied with anything if you don't try this." But when I told Dr. Brant, she shook her head gravely and said, "Remember your Thomas Wolfe." I knew that she was referring to the famous dictum that you can't go home again, but I thought Wolfe was only one man and Darcy Anne Titwell Brant only one woman. That they had found it impossible did not mean that I would, so I smiled and said, "It's not exactly that," though of course it was, and cut the conversation short, disappointed because I had wanted her bracing approval and interest. Her small book on the Caskill family sits on my nightstand and I am still slightly in awe of her.

Osier College had asked me down for an interview. I flew to Lexington and took the bus south, watching the summer landscape flower white and green with a softness that day like mist.

"My mom told me he was no good and I wouldn't listen," a young pregnant woman said bitterly to her seatmate, an elderly woman who clucked understandingly.

A voice behind me said, "So I got her recipe for bread and butter pickles and it turned out real good."

"He's on something," a man was saying across his seat back to the elderly woman, who shook her head.

"Went into the hospital on Wednesday and Thursday she was dead."

"My granddaddy worked in that mine."

"I couldn't find me a job so I come on home."

When my mother told her parents in Osierville that I was coming, they said they hoped I would stay with them, which surprised us both. I was both reluctant and curious. We had spent so little time with them in my childhood. Grandfather Elliott, a doctor, had retired about three years ago, and Grandmother was ailing, confined to a wheelchair. They lived in a white-painted brick house on the outskirts of town, up a little street that ended abruptly at the foot of a hill, as most of Osierville's streets do. Green shutters and green lawn fringed with marshaled roses. My mother's parents have always hired someone else to keep the lawn smooth, the plants healthy, someone like my second cousin Billy Caskill, who makes a living keeping lawn and garden for other people.

They had always spent many of their weekends visiting relatives in Lexington—people known to me only as senders of Christmas cards. I asked my mother why they didn't move to Lexington when the doctor retired. "I think they just got used to doing it this way," she said. "They've been thinking of themselves as exiles for so long that it's a way of life." Lately she had become quite solicitous of them, and I knew she and Daddy had made a special trip to celebrate the doctor's seventy-fifth birthday.

When I was a child in Kentucky, Daddy had been reluctant to visit them, probably because they always talked about such things as Cousin James Elliott's new judgeship and a dinner party they had attended in Lexington and a concert for which they had traveled to Cincinnati. I asked Mommy once why she hadn't given way and taken me to see them, leaving Daddy behind, although I was glad that she hadn't, because they always acted as though Daddy wasn't there anyhow. "I might have found the situation too comfortable," she replied, giving me the glance direct. An honest woman, my mother. Elliptical, but honest. A woman who herself likes the glossy ads in *The New Yorker* and classical music and giving dinners. (As does her daughter.) When the Caskills wanted to visit each other, they just dropped by, and the woman of the house started preparing food if it was anywhere near mealtime and even if it wasn't. But Mommy invited people to dinner. If you dropped by, you'd get some chips and dip maybe, but for dinner you had to be invited. She would start cooking the day before, marinating meat perhaps, or baking one of her flourless chocolate cakes, or both. A thick white tablecloth—a gift from Grandmother Elliott—went on the plain pine table, and if it was warm weather, some of her irises or yellow roses or zinnias graced it.

About once a year, the Elliotts would come to dinner in their dark blue Buick. (Every five years they traded it in for a new dark blue Buick.) Grandfather Elliott invariably wore a suit and Grandmother a dressy blouse and skirt. Nobody seemed to say anything much. We couldn't even talk about politics, because the Elliotts were fervent Republicans. And certainly not about religion. The Elliotts were Episcopalians. I can just imagine Grandpa Orson saying, "What's that when it's to home?" But if he said something like that, it was probably in one of those low-voiced conversations that the men of our family carry on with their wives before they go to sleep or before they, and here my forebears would have me draw a curtain. It's a custom of which I do not wholly disapprove.

Dr. Elliott opened the door when I, aspiring college teacher, rang the bell, his face gaunt beneath still-thick gray hair, and bid me enter with grave courtesy. Dressed as I remembered him, in a dark suit and tie, he was a little stooped now, and beneath bushy eyebrows his eyes, a little rheumy, were judgmental, though, I was to discover, not necessarily disapproving. Grandmother was napping until dinnertime, he said. Gracie, the woman who had worked for them for many years, came in from the kitchen at his call and silently took me upstairs to the guest room, wiping her hands on the apron that mostly hid her cheap print dress. The large mirror on the dark dresser shone at me immaculately. There was a white spread on the bed and yellow roses on the small nightstand. "The flowers were yore Mamaw's idea," Gracie said and left me there. Dominated thrillingly by the hills framing the windows, I put down my bags and freshened up in the spotless bathroom.

When I rejoined my grandfather in the spotless living room, we made small talk about my trip, about the weather, about the lone Italian restaurant that had opened last month, something new in Osierville. There were pauses. Suddenly he said, "Your father's a good man."

"I think so," I said lightly, not knowing how to respond. Was he aware then how much I had always resented their treatment of Daddy? He seemed somehow disappointed: to wait for me to say something more.

I asked him if he missed his practice. "I wish I hadn't given it up so soon," he said. "I'm used to being a busy man. I run into my patients all the time, and they say they miss me." My grandparents' long argument with my mother, and by extension with my father, as to their not-so-innocent snobbery had obscured for me the fact that Dr. Elliott led a busy and useful life, respected, perhaps liked, by his patients.

Grandmother, a little woman with brilliant white hair and limpid blue eyes surprisingly large in her oval face, was gracious when she wheeled in to join us for dinner, her arthritic, gnarled hands reaching upward to pull me down in an awkward, unexpected embrace. I told her that I enjoyed the roses.

"Your mother always liked the yellow roses best," she said. The roses in my parents' backyard were various shades of yellow. (I always liked the yellow and pink of the Helen Hayes.)

Over the dinner of roast chicken and vegetables, Grandfather told me that the fresh tomatoes came from Gracie's garden. He added, "I don't know when she finds time to tend it." Gracie was within hearing distance in the kitchen and he could just as well have asked her. "I think her husband takes care of it," my grandmother said in a low voice. "She goes home Sundays," Dr. Elliott said, "but she wouldn't work in the garden on Sunday. She goes to church." I felt an urge to call Gracie in and ask her about her gardening arrangements but I stifled it.

Before I went to bed, I tried to call my parents on my cell phone, but the hills cut off the signal. As I dropped off to sleep, I felt the solid, reassuring presence of those hills, something of childhood's heedless peace.

The next morning, I was interviewed by Osier College's English Department chairman at breakfast at the Hilltop Inn, located on the other side of Osierville. To get the feel of a place, you have to walk, and the inn was within walking distance. I have always been a walker; the nooks and crannies of time elude the automobile. Hilltop Inn lay practically straight across and up, up. Most of the houses I passed were small compared to the Elliott house, and they sat on small, slanted yards. I saw a teenage boy mowing a particularly slanted one and admired his application of high energy to the hand-operated lawnmower. He stopped to observe me passing. A woman rocking on a porch said, "Howdy," and a passing couple smiled at me.

Professor Isaly was short and sixtyish. His round face, beneath a bald dome, was dominated by a wide, pleasant mouth. Small, mild eyes met mine as he rose to draw back my chair. He asked me if I had found a good place to stay, and when I told him I was staying with my grandparents, he said,

"Oh, yes, I've met Dr. Elliott. I hear he was an excellent doctor." I wanted to ask him if he had liked my grandfather but of course I didn't. "I had had the impression that your people lived farther out of town," he continued, and when I told him my father's folks lived near Sarvis Mountain, his kind, piggy eyes gleamed approvingly. "Many of our students live in town," he said, "and a few go home to places like Maryland and even New Jersey. But most of them come from rural places right here in a three-county area. So do a few of Osier's faculty members. You'll have to meet Johnny Busbey, who would be a colleague of yours if you joined us. Johnny comes from the Sarvis Creek area. This is his second year as an instructor."

Then he got down to business. He told me about the heavy course schedule, the tiny salary, the drug problem. From time to time we replenished our coffee cups from the carafe standing on the counter. I was charmed by that public carafe, by the familiar twang in the voices of other diners, and I felt divided between them and Dr. Isaly's reasoned academic voice. (He himself was from Louisville, an urban man.) He wound up soon afterward, giving me a schedule of appointments, looking at his watch, saying he had another appointment. I wondered with what rival. I wondered if I had displeased him. He really had not asked me a great deal about myself, though he had obviously listened critically to my responses and questions. After he left, I lingered in the Hilltop restaurant, having yet another cup of coffee, watching a part of my past I had never experienced. There did not seem to be much for me to explore, used as I was now to the cosmopolitan busyness of Chicago. I saw Osierville as a hologram, a oneness that required little internal knowledge to be either accepted or rejected. Lunchtime came around and I was still sitting there. I beckoned to the waiter, a diminutive girl who furtively removed her feet from the unsuitable shoes she was wearing and rubbed her left foot against her right ankle when she thought no one was watching. She brought herself in my direction, her tiny, pale face intent beneath a thatch of brown hair. I asked her if she was a student at the university and she giggled, "No, ma'am," as though I'd suggested something outlandish. The Hilltop Inn had what seemed to be the best fried oysters I had ever eaten. Like a schoolgirl playing hooky, I ordered a milkshake to go with them.

After lunch, I checked the mental map that Grandfather Elliott had provided me with, and made my way up, up to campus, past more small white houses with carefully tended lawns and out-of-date cars sitting here and there on the street, and then past university buildings, red brick with peeling white trim, higher than the houses and with larger lawns. I met Olivia Hamilton, one of the tenured English faculty, in a dusty building full of deserted classrooms. She was dressed in a ginger-colored suit and spike heels. Her black hair was pulled back in a large bun, and she wore hoop earrings. "I just got back from London," she said smugly as she settled behind a scarred wooden desk. Behind her were shelves full of Shakespeare and Victorian literature. Dr. Isaly had said that she was a very good teacher, one who knew how to keep the students interested. The boys undoubtedly lusted after her, I thought, and the girls wanted to be like her.

"This is not a school that claims much attention elsewhere," she said, "but we have wonderful students. You'd find most of them diffident and courteous and likable."

I spoke briefly about my own Kentucky attachments, about Sarvis Creek and the Caskills, and she was enthusiastic about what I might have to offer while at the same time quizzing me on my academic qualifications. We spoke for about an hour and a half, the last thirty minutes spent on her trip to London and my life in Chicago. Olivia was to become my best friend in town, and I always found it disconcerting that she was not a Kentuckian. That day, however, I felt in league with her, united in a common difference.

She took me down the hall and introduced me to the

Boltons, an older married couple who had been teaching at Osier forever, having come to eastern Kentucky in the sixties from upstate New York. They had been Vista volunteers, and their pride in their youthful commitment and venturesomeness seemed to still sustain them. Olivia had said that between them they had taught practically every course in the English Department over the years. "Of course, there are more of us now," she said, "and we are more specialized." As generalists, the Boltons were enthusiastic about freshman composition and the sophomore literature survey that I might be teaching. It turned out that they had in effect chosen the texts I would be using. I was disappointed to hear that there *was* a text for the literature survey, since I had had my own idea about works that I would like to use. However, I kept this to myself and listened to their gentle memoirs, pleased by his thin, tall courtliness and her short, plump vivacity and, more importantly, by their seriousness of purpose.

My last interview proved to be with a Lexingtonian who taught seventeenth-century literature and philosophy of literature, an awkward fellow with a buzz haircut who emphasized that the position would probably not lead to "anything better." He looked disappointed himself. By the time I left his dingy office and crossed the campus's thick green grass, it was nearly dusk and there was a purple hue to the encircling hills. I wondered what on earth I was doing there.

My grandparents were waiting for me in their living room. "Gracie's made a good dinner," Grandmother Elliott said, handing me a glass of wine. We never had wine or liquor at home except on those rare occasions when Daddy got himself a little pickled. "Don't you miss it?" I had asked Mommy. "I don't really like it," she replied dismissively. I did like it, and I sipped merlot now while they asked me how my day had gone. Grandfather Elliott said approvingly that Professor Isaly was well respected in town. They didn't know any of the others. "Though I recognize Mrs. Hamilton when I see her,"

Grandfather said with lurking appreciation. My grandmother gave him a look.

Dinner was a Virginia ham with fresh garden things and a raspberry cobbler for dessert. "Gracie freezes the berries and brings them out when she wants them," Grandmother said. I smiled at Gracie, who did not smile back. When she returned to the kitchen, my grandmother said furtively, pushing a strand of silvered hair behind a pearly ear, "She just lost her brother last week. Killed in an accident. He was a truck driver." It troubled me that my first day in Osierville was punctuated by talk of drugs and death. I had wanted a day of beauty but I had met with complexities and ironies and dingy offices.

There was no time during that first trip to Osierville to visit Grandma Sarah Beth and Aunt Tessie and Uncle Floyd. I had written a letter to them telling Grandma that the trip would be a quick one since I had to get back to my part-time job in Chicago. I knew how proud she would be about her granddaughter the professor (in her eyes). What a feast she and Aunt Tessie would have set out. I could have visited the store, too, and talked to Uncle Floyd about the pros and cons of the current incumbent at the White House.

When I awoke at six the next morning in the Elliott house, I could see out my window the morning mists swathing the mountains, islanding the town, and I pictured Sarah Beth somewhere in the middle of those mists and knew I would take the job if it was offered.

Downstairs, Gracie had coffee ready, and Grandfather insisted on taking me to the bus station, where a group of somber morning people waited for the bus. (The one-room station with its tattered posters wasn't open yet.) As I joined the other customers, my grandfather and I were suddenly shy with each other, but he insisted on staying until the bus arrived.

I called Cheu when I got back to Chicago. The city was in the middle of a heat wave. Cheu fed me dinner—he had a repertoire of five or six dishes, a mixture of Asian and American.

We started with a spring salad, cool and cucumbery, and he poured me a glass of chilled Pinot Grigio. "Will you come and visit if I get the job?" I said impulsively and then regretted it. Cheu didn't have a lot of money. He squeezed my hand and spoke the phrase he had picked up at a movie—he loved westerns, an anomaly in a nonviolent man—"You betcha." We smiled, thoroughly understanding each other. It's a marvel that Cheu and I never had an amorous passage. I guess we relied on each other too much for that. Now he's gone, all the way back to South Korea.

When Dr. Isaly wrote to tell me I was hired, I called Grandma Sarah Beth and then my parents immediately after. Daddy was ecstatic. "We'll give you a chance to get settled," he said, "before we come down."

"Are you sure you want to do this?" Mommy asked.

"I can always leave at the end of the year," I rejoined, hearing the relief in my voice, although my major plan was to stay for the five years that my contract was renewable and then see what was what.

Within two weeks, I had sublet my small apartment and packed and had a yard sale in the courtyard. Jennifer and Ben threw me a party at Ben's North Side condo (stainless steel kitchen appliances and overlooking the lake). Cheu and his current girlfriend came, as did the physics major that I had been half-heartedly dating. They gave me a watch with which to get to my classes on time and a beautifully illustrated map of Kentucky. The latter, with its scrolls and delicate colors, fit perfectly with my Kentucky mythology, but didn't look like Osierville had looked when I saw it last.

What I wasn't expecting was the courtly letter I received two or three days later from Grandfather Elliott, inviting me to make my home with them. I was used to being on my own now, I thought, and I might make friends my grandparents wouldn't approve of. But, on the other hand, I had reluctantly liked them on my visit, and living with them would be true Kentucky, true family—and cheap. I slept on it and then doubtfully called my mother. What did she think? I was expecting her to say don't do that, but she didn't. "It'll please them a lot," she said. "And my mother needs cheering up. She was always a busy woman, and that wheelchair is killing her."

"What about me?" I asked, like a child. Her child.

"Well, don't do it if it'll make you unhappy. You'd save some money, though."

"I always thought you didn't care for them that much."

"Well, guess again."

"Do you like yellow roses best?"

"Yes, didn't you know that?"

"I guess. Grandmother Elliott told me anyhow."

"You're not going to call her *that*, are you?"

"No, I just call her Grandmother."

"Her name is Cassie," my mother added tartly.

"I knew that." It seemed an informal name for Grandmother Elliott.

I wrote back to Grandfather (Richard), accepting their offer and thanking them. But when I returned to Osier County, I went first to visit Grandma Sarah Beth, who had written asking if I wanted to stay with her and Tessie and Floyd until I found a place in town.

Grandma Sarah Beth is a ladylike woman, wearing always simple cotton dresses, usually ones that she has made, for she is still a fine seamstress. Her figure used to be neatly rounded, and her face is reasonably pleasing and always in full view— her gray hair pulled back from it into a large bun at the nape of her neck. But what I have noticed most about her are her large, mild eyes that will, when she is excited, suddenly become dense with gray light. Her voice quickens, too, and suddenly you are in the presence of someone who has engulfed the mild lady to whom you were speaking the moment before.

Her house's interior was created by her, still has kerosene lamps in the living room that are used from time to time for a quiet evening of talking, the television off, as my father says it was so often even in the early sixties when Grandpa Orson brought it new into their home. One wall is covered with family pictures, in the Kentucky way, including daguerreotypes of Sarah Beth's grandfather and grandmother. Grandpa Orson's family is represented, too. Great-uncles and great-aunts, aunts, uncles, cousins, weddings, funerals, birthdays, family reunions, school pictures. Each year the wall becomes a little more crowded. When we go to visit, Daddy looks at it critically and says, "Mommy, it's time to start another wall."

She has also created a small library in the living room. The northern wall supports bookshelves that Grandpa Orson had planed down and varnished many years before his death. Two shelves are taken up by church bulletins, some dating back to the 1920s. There is a heavy old Bible—King James version, of course—in which she has recorded family events, births, weddings, deaths. My grandmother takes her religion seriously. But she is nonetheless rebellious concerning church matters, particularly those that relegate women to a secondary place. Which pleases me.

When in my Kentucky childhood I said I might want to become an airline pilot—or, at another time, depending upon what I was reading, an explorer or an actress, say—her eyes would fill with light and we would discuss the pros and cons of that particular job. She approves of Mommy's teaching and defers to her daughter-in-law Bernice in matters she considers to be what I would now call "scholarly." (There is nothing wrong with her own mind, except now a little forgetfulness.)

But in matter having to do with a good yarn, Grandma and I are the ones who made our way through the volumes of Dickens and Jane Austen that I found in the school library. "When I was young," she tells me, "the school didn't have a library. The county let the school borrow a few books from time to time and when the wagon came around I was first in line."

She put me in the spare bedroom that had been my father's. On the wall were his high school diploma and two certificates of recognition that he had received from the Osier County Democratic Party. In the old bookcase, *Treasure Island* and *The Five Little Peppers and How They Grew* were still there. On the inside cover of the latter was a sheet of paper with colored scrolls stating that Daddy had received it for good conduct in the sixth grade. Grandma appeared in the doorway and said, "I always keep some of his things in this room." When she came over and hugged me again, I saw that she was now shorter than I was. One of her quilts, log cabin pattern, was on the bed, and a rag rug she had made lay on the floor. I hugged her back and cried a little over her shoulder. "The house looks good," I said, and it did, the dark old furniture providing shade in the sunny rooms.

It was four o'clock and in an hour evening would set in, as the sun went quickly down behind the hills. "Tessie keeps it spick-and-span now," Grandma said wistfully. "But I'm getting supper tonight." In her letter she had promised me a fried chicken dinner, and we had it that first evening. Golden fried chicken and mashed potatoes and Grandma's tangy, salty chicken gravy and string beans, and cornbread to crumble in the gravy, and banana pudding for dessert.

Floyd had come home from the store, and sure enough, we talked about politics (our presidential candidate was trailing), and we talked about Tessie and Floyd's children, my cousins, what were they doing now, and about Tessie's garden, and about Aunt Charlene and my parents and the twins, and about John Ritchie's death and Minerva Jones's heart attack and Sam Alseck Jr.'s new house—and about Grandpa Orson. Tomorrow, Grandma would take me up on the graveyard to visit him. After supper, we sat on the porch and talked some more. Night set in and fireflies, lightning bugs, voyaged in the yard.

When the time came for me to move into Osierville and

assume my teaching duties, Uncle Floyd loaded up my luggage and took me there. As we parked in front of my new home, Grandfather Elliott, whom I had called before leaving Sarvis Creek, came out and offered his hand to Uncle Floyd and said, "Hello. Come on in the house and have something cool to drink before you leave." Floyd carried my luggage in, though I protested I could do it. He took off his cap and greeted Grandmother awkwardly and said to Grandfather that he had to be getting back. Gracie came in, and he said, "Howdy, Grace. How's your brother's wife?" Then he was gone, and I was alone with two strangers who just happened to be my grandparents. There were more yellow roses in the bedroom.

On Monday, the English Department held a meeting. We were seated in flimsy folding chairs around a plain table. Box lunches had been provided, and there was coffee brewing in the corner on an enamel-top table by a small sink, which had a slightly rusty look. The president of the college, a burly man who had come to Osierville after holding a deanship in Maryland, talked of the students as though they were slightly diseased specimens. I took an immediate dislike to him. When I was introduced, people came over to say hello. The Lexingtonian looked as though he wanted to offer his condolences. Olivia Hamilton whispered, "Every year I say I'm going to skip this, but of course I don't." She had Johnny Busbey in tow. Remembering that he was from my neck of the woods, I looked curiously at him, a dark-haired fellow with dangling arms and a sweet, diffident smile. He greeted me shyly, and I said, "You're from Sarvis Creek. Me too." He nodded. "Johnny's going to show you the ropes tomorrow," Olivia said.

Johnny and I met early the next morning, in intoxicatingly fresh air with a faintly damp edge to it, in front of the building that housed the English office. In the role of teacher, he proved more forthcoming, and we were soon chatting a little. Not about Sarvis Creek, though. I got my schedule for the five classes I was going to teach, Mondays through Fridays, classes every weekday. "No use to schedule Saturday classes," he said. "We're lucky if they're here Friday afternoons."

By the time we got to the bookstore, after lunching together on High Street, down the hill, at the Osier Grill (all recipes with a savory amount of fat except the pinto beans and the self-conscious chef's salad), we were talking about who was from what part of Sarvis Creek and which people do you know? Johnny lived near the mouth of the creek, where it debouched into the river, so our intimate locales were different, but he had an uncle who traded at Grandpa's store (still considered Orson Caskill's by local citizens), and one of his older sisters knew Tessie and Floyd's son Martin. I remembered Johnny's Uncle Forest: a big, genial miner who liked to tell Daddy tall tales.

But Johnny was reticent about himself. Olivia, a close friend of his, subsequently told me he was gay and that I should keep that bit of news to myself. Months later he confided in me that his father had beaten him for it and turned him out of the house. He had lived with his mother's sister until he got the job at Osier.

My classes were too large and too much the same but different enough to require different readings and different assignments. The students were for the most part friendly and they talked with that twang that was inexpressibly harmonious to me: utterly familiar and yet strange. Of all my students, I loved Donald, who was not so quick but whose personal journal was full of curiosity and affection for people and animals and nature in general. His journal entries got better and better as the year progressed, but he never seemed to pay attention in class, sitting in the back row in the south corner, by the windows, his small figure slumped into the uncomfortable chair. I wanted to commune with this being with whom I felt such unexpected kinship. But he never met my eyes, never said "Bye" as he left the class, as several of his classmates did.

In two months, I was exhausted. Olivia said, "Pace yourself, for God's sake." We had lunch together once or twice a week. She provided helpful guidance and told me about her childhood in Minnesota and her tempestuous life before meeting her husband. I was a little shocked about her liaisons with married men, whom she seemed formerly to have preferred. "Oh, you're a Kentucky girl, all right," she laughed. "Small-town Minnesota is just the same, of course. But the times they are a-changing."

Mostly I worked and worked and worked. My students were late and sloppy and eager for life and bored. They were crazy about movies and TV shows, and their lives were far different from those of their parents, or perhaps I should say their grandparents. I smelled grass in the air every day, and I was sure two or three of my students were hooked on something stronger, judging by their pallid faces and dilated pupils. When they came to my office, they were often anxious and tired. So was I. Often there was an air of mutual sympathy in the room.

In October, the weather was unseasonably hot, and there was no air conditioning in the brick and concrete dorms. Or in my office, in a small frame building of dubious vintage (I could smell the mold, and there were yellowjackets close by). Sue Anne, another student that I cared about, came in one day to tell me that her mother was sick and she had to go home for a week or two. I asked her where Raccoon Creek was, and it turned out that it was not far from the place that had been owned by Grandpa Orson's cousin Andy and now belonged to one of Andy's daughters and her husband. I made out assignments for Sue Anne. "I don't know if I'll have time," she added doubtfully.

"Please try, Sue. You're a bright young woman, and I don't want you to fall behind."

She flushed with pleasure. "You really thank I'm smart?"

I nodded my head and said inadequately, "Tell your mom I hope she feels better soon."

She gave me a sad smile as she left my office. I felt for the first time the power a teacher might come to have.

Occasionally I made time to go to Sarvis Creek for Sunday supper with Grandma Sarah Beth and Tessie and Floyd. Usually one or two of my cousins were there, and we made a start toward getting reacquainted. My favorite was Martin, who is older than I. He has a job as mine electrician, and his wife, April Jane, teaches elementary school. They both proved to have a wry sense of humor and a healthy skepticism about mainstream America. April Jane baked the world's best lemon meringue pie. "The family that eats together stays together," she quipped, which has always been considered a sound rule in eastern Kentucky.

I went home to Ohio for the holidays. My mother let me recuperate, doing almost all the Christmas baking herself. My father was working overtime at GM and looked tired. He was wistful about Osier County. The twins decorated the tree and bought shiny gifts for everyone. I sent the latest Silas House novel to Grandma Sarah Beth, a silky blouse for Tessie to wear to church, and a history of labor unions to Floyd. The Elliotts and I had exchanged gifts before I left Kentucky. They gave me a warm winter robe and a subscription to *The New Yorker*. I reciprocated with a vase that came from a potter in Berea. We drank sherry the evening before I left.

Back in Osierville a little early, I began preparing for the new semester. Cheu was coming and I wanted some free time for that weekend. He came on the bus from Lexington, emerging bright-eyed and interested. This was definitely not Chicago. He brought greetings, a pair of garnet earrings from himself, and an antique bed warmer from Jennifer and Stephen. He also brought an international, cosmopolitan aura, and I appreciated almost immediately that, marginal though Cheu might be in Chicago, he was still sophisticated and very urbane. I told him I was worried about the tenuousness of my relationship with my students, and he replied, "It's probably your wish to be one of them that is hindering you."

My grandparents asked if he would like to use the sofa in the living room. Cheu told me he would be too self-conscious parked in a stranger's living room, so he stayed at the one hotel in town, which mostly catered to families of the college students. Friday evening, we ate dinner with the Elliotts. Grandfather wanted to hear about life in South Korea and India. He was genuinely interested, and Cheu was more talkative on these topics than I had ever heard him be.

On Saturday, we went to Sarvis Creek. Cheu was instantly appreciative of the hills and of Grandma Sarah Beth, who showed him her collection of books on Kentucky and told him about the ways things were in her childhood. Tessie and Floyd were quiet and a little distant. Cheu hugged Sarah Beth when we left, and she hugged him back. "You come visit us again," she said, patting his narrow shoulder, and he increased the strength of his hug.

"Are you coming back to Chicago?" Cheu asked when I took him to the bus station early Monday morning. "I don't know," I said uneasily. "If I don't stay here, though, I'll be back." Until Cheu came, I had not been certain about this. I still thought I might stay at Osier, but if I didn't, I had toyed with the idea of spending a year in Paris. Too far away, my subconscious had evidently decided.

January was a dreary, cold month. The classrooms were either overheated or draftily cold. Grandmother Cassie had a relapse and spent most of the month in Osier Hospital. Knowing firsthand, no doubt, all the things that could go wrong, and, I'm sure, feeling like a pilot that had relinquished the controls, Grandfather spent too many wakeful nights in the hospital and came down with the flu, which at his age was no joke. Gracie was everybody's mainstay. She and I found moments now to talk about our families and about her garden, but Gracie would grow distant when either of the grandparents came within hearing. She told me one day when

Grandfather was at the hospital that the job was very important to her. She was the main support for her mother and aunt
as well as for her own family. Her husband had been out of
work for two years.

In late January, Grandmother came home and Grandfather
instantly threw off his remaining symptoms. That week, several students had appointments to discuss their research
papers. I was surprised on Thursday when Donald, whom I
had taught the previous semester, came into my office. I had
praised his creative work highly but had given him a B-minus
because his other work was slightly below average or perhaps
more than slightly. He had not come to the final day of classes
(we had lumped two class periods together and were watching
Kenneth Branagh's *Much Ado About Nothing*, which regrettably
is what some students thought it was). He sat there silently,
his thick brown hair shaggy over his ears, flopping on his thin,
melancholy face, hands spread out on top of his thighs, gray
eyes looking past me out the window. He was a slight boy and
did not occupy the whole chair. Finally, I said lightly, "And
what brings you here today, Donald?"

"They told me I gotta leave school," he said in a burst. "My
grades are too low."

"That's too bad. I'm sorry, Donald. What will you do?"

"I can't leave school. My grandparents don't want me
back."

"What about your parents?"

"Mom died and Dad took off for Columbus. We don't even
know if he's still there. He *said* he'd send for me."

I asked him if he were sure his grandparents wouldn't
have him back.

"They told me after they caught me using stuff the second
time. They made me pack all my things and bring them to
Osier with me. They kept the table Mommy left me. I got her
other things, though." He looked up at me. "I thought maybe
you would help me."

"What kind of stuff did they find you with?" I asked, knowing I was getting beyond my experience and know-how. I had taught one quarter in a Chicago community college, and some of my students there had probably been on drugs, but none had ever confided that to me. One of Donald's classmates in high school had given him a taste for OxyContin, he said, but now he was using crack cocaine. "Who gets it for you, Donald?" I asked, dreading the answer because I would have to do something about it.

He stood up. "I don't want that kind of trouble," he said. "I'm not telling you that."

"Are you sure it's not because you don't want to cut off your supply?"

"This ain't what I came to you for," he cried. "Promise me you won't tell anybody."

I said I couldn't do that, but then he looked at me with such agony that I hesitated.

He seized the moment. "I'll get help," he said. "I promise I'll get help."

I hesitated even longer. He made as if to go. I beckoned to him and opened up the school directory. "If we get you reinstated, will you call this number and make an appointment?"

"I promise," he said fervently, his thin shoulders hunched forward like inverted wings.

"I'm not sure I can do anything. I'm new here myself, but I'll try."

"They told me I just missed making probation," he said pleadingly.

"Okay. You call me here tomorrow. Do you understand, Donald? Tomorrow or I'll send someone to look for you."

"I'll call," he said, hurrying to the door. "I'll call."

I telephoned Dr. Isaly, and, fortunately, I got hold of him right away. I told him about Donald's unusual creative potential, but I didn't tell him about the drugs. He said he would take the matter up with the dean of students, but he wouldn't be able to talk to him before Monday. The dean was going to be tied up in a weekend seminar in Lexington. "I realize," he said kindly, "that you don't want Mr. Jordan to miss too much of this semester. With his needs, that would be drastic."

Donald did call during my Friday office hours. He sounded thoughtful and distant. He promised he would call again on Monday. On Saturday he killed himself. It took up most of the front page of the Sunday paper, which is how I found out. One of the things his dad had left behind was a gun. Donald had been carrying it for months, his friend said. Nobody said anything about drugs. Donald had stuck the gun in his mouth sitting on a commode in a locked bathroom.

I threw up on the breakfast table. Grandfather Elliott brought paper towels and a cool, damp cloth. "I know that boy," I whispered, pointing to the vomit-streaked newspaper. "I talked to him Thursday."

Grandfather got the story out of me and then said, "You'll have to tell them what you know." It was reassuring to have him reinforce my conscience. So I told them about the drugs and about Donald's illegal presence in the dorm. The day after I contacted the police, my own story appeared in the town newspaper. The following week, Dr. Isaly called me in to tell me that the college president didn't want me to return the following year. "I'm sorry," Dr. Isaly said, "but once your prior knowledge came out in the newspaper, the president felt we hadn't much choice. I understand your dilemma and think with a little more experience you would have handled the situation differently. But there's nothing I can do."

I had begun to consider leaving anyhow but to leave like this, a failure. The Elliotts were kind and supportive and indignant for me, but I felt I would be leaving with Donald's blood on my hands. I felt I had disgraced my relatives.

I got through the rest of the school year. My students found out that I was leaving in disgrace and three of them came to my office and asked if I wanted their class to stage a protest. They were vocal and sweet, as though my new condition somehow made me one of them. Sue Anne showed up one day with a freshly baked stack cake. (I had expressed an interest in her mother's recipe.) Olivia talked to the president, but he was adamant.

Before I left Osier County, I went to spend two weeks with Grandma Sarah Beth. The grandparents Elliott saw me off as though I were going to a foreign country. (Grandfather Elliott offered to come and pick me up after my stay on Sarvis Creek and deposit me at the bus station, but Tessie had already volunteered Floyd for that.) I left Osier College telling myself that anyhow I was not saintly enough to remain, that the students demanded more than I would be willing to give. And it was true that I was attached to habits I had learned to treasure elsewhere. To stay now seemed to limit the horizon, to threaten claustrophobia. Yet I was overwhelmed with sadness.

On the Saturday after classes ended, Floyd arrived in his fifteen-year-old pickup, which only his mechanic skills kept running. Its right fender was heavily dented from where a tree had fallen on it during a spring storm one year, it was generally in need of new paint, and its engine was harsh. Feeling unable to call, I had written a brief note to Grandma Sarah Beth saying that I would be leaving and that it was not my choice, although I might have left anyhow. She had managed to get hold of me on my uncertain cell phone. "You just needed some seasoning, Melissa," she said thoughtfully, not condemning the president out of hand. "It's a pity. Why don't you try Berea next?" (She knew that I had a real ambition to teach at Berea, a good school that offered a grand work-study program for mountain students and which had practiced what we now called "civil rights" from its inception.) "I'm not ready for them, Grandma. And even if I were, I don't know that they'd consider me once they heard from Osier." Though it was true that Dr. Isaly and Olivia had assured me that they would give me good recommendations, and so had

Johnny ("for what's it worth," he said with his usual diffi-
dence). Dr. Isaly's reaction had pretty much been the same as
Sarah Beth's: that I needed "seasoning."

I wasn't sure I wanted to teach at all. The horror of
Donald's death overrode me.

After my stay at the Elliotts, the Caskill house seemed
smaller and shabbier than I had thought it to be. Before, it
had never occurred to me to compare it with houses in Ohio
or Chicago, as though that would be comparing apples and
oranges. Again I was in my father's old bedroom. I felt nostalgia for my parents' past, for my own past with them there. I
felt I had failed my father too.

It was mid-May, and there were things to be done in the
garden. (We were already eating lettuce and onions, lettuce
fresh from the garden with green onions cut into it, sprinkled
with salt with hot bacon grease grizzled onto it, the whole
eaten right away before the grease cools.) Tessie and I hoed
the beans and the tomatoes and the potatoes and the corn and
the carrot ridges and the melons and I forget what else. By
the end of the day, my arms would be sore and my back, what
with weeding thrown in, aching. My body had forgotten how
this felt, but now it remembered.

While we were busying ourselves in the garden, somewhere among those hours of respite, I felt my past catch up
with me. Kentucky was no longer an eternal spring, but it
was Sarah Beth and Orson's patch of earth, where the sun
shone on me in unmythical heat. Then we would come into
the shade, to the hearty supper that Grandma Sarah Beth had
prepared, Uncle Floyd joining us from the store. After supper, Tessie and I would do the dishes. The house had running
water now. Floyd had laid the pipes from the deep well out
back by the Red Delicious tree that had been there since God
only knew when. Then I would join Grandma on the front
porch, while Tessie joined Floyd in the living room to watch
TV. I resented the sound of it edging out onto the front porch,

spoiling the whippoorwill's call. Grandma and I watched the lightning bugs (Ohio's fireflies) and talked about family and the past. I felt that old closeness, as though we were more like each other than anybody else in the world. Our passion was the same at root, however it might mutate. I told her I had failed. Looking at me carefully, she said tartly, "You treated that young man like a human being. You can call that being a failure if you want to."

"He might still be alive if I'd gotten professional help right away."

"So next time you'll know."

"They're sending me away, Grandma. There won't be a next time."

"There's always a next time. If not in one place, then in another. Live and learn, Melissa. That's all we can do." We sat silently for a few minutes, and then she said, "When your daddy was young, Orson and I had a big argument. I found out he'd been seeing another woman. I told him I'd leave him. I remember we were talking in bed after the children were asleep and we kept our voices down so they wouldn't hear." (She looks at me to determine whether I'm old enough to hear this.) "He begged me not to leave and I said I didn't know but right now I couldn't stand the sight of him. He said I didn't need to leave, he'd leave himself. He got up and threw some things into a suitcase and said he'd stay with his brother— Darryl, you know. I told the young'uns the next morning that he'd left early to stay with Darryl to help out with building the new room that Darryl and Lily were adding to their house. Charlene looked at me funny, but whatever she thought, she didn't say anything. Then Orson came up with a better solution. He came to the house and asked me if I'd forgiven him and I said no so he said he guessed he'd better go visit family in Detroit. The kids bought that, like you young'uns say now, though Char still looked funny. So he went, but I wrote to him the next week and told him to come home."

I looked up from my seat on the upper porch steps to my bent grandmother in the rocking chair. We still shared, after all, Sarah Beth and I, a belief that Kentucky was somehow a magical medium in whose light we were suspended as though in spun glass. I felt the terror of impending loss. She smiled at me now in what I believed to be utter comprehension. "I went to your second cousin Bobby's office last week and had him help me make out my will. I left you one-third of the place."

Shocked with pleasure and responsibility, I blurted, "I'll probably never come back here to stay, Grandma."

"But you'll always come back for a while," my grandmother said, and her voice was both a statement and a command.

I wondered what Orson had felt visiting his brother in Detroit. Had he been excited by being within easy distance of a large city (his brother lived in a suburb where a lot of other Kentuckians had settled) or had he been homesick and heartsick? I pictured him in Rome then, my young, tall grandfather, his hair brown then and his eyes perhaps a softer hazel than I had known them, fighting a war and then coming back to the green circle of hills. Had he felt claustrophobic, or had he sung to himself that old song "K-e-n-t-u-c-k-y spells Kentucky but it means Paradise"? But then there was Fergus, and Fergus was nobody's idea of paradise, except perhaps for a few women who soon changed their minds. Saul Bellow once wrote something like the impossibility of losing yourself in an idealistic stratosphere in Chicago. The radiator always creaked, he said. Fergus was Grandpa Orson's creaking radiator, I suppose, or rather a dark compass that was the shadow of true north. And then there was poverty and uncertain work and a world that was disappearing, as all our worlds must disappear, but drastically so. But my grandfather stood tall and straight and dealt with it, no doubt with a certain ironic detachment. He had learned early perhaps that nothing lasts forever, and he had married Sarah Beth, who had made their world a rich one, with his connivance and, I was sure, with his blessing. I honor them. Lying here in Hyde Park, watching the moon float above the white dome of the Museum of Science and Industry and the dreams of tomorrow afloat in my willing mind, I know that I have not yet found my niche but that going home again was a movement toward true north.

Perhaps I belong to no one place; to all the places I have been and those to which I will go. But I have learned that Osier County is my *sine qua non* and that of the people I love most, whom Darcy Anne Titwell calls the Sunday People—not because they sometimes or often attend a church but because they are preoccupied with meanings ancient and modern, because they believe the eternal questions of landscape and community, life and death are of great value.

Acknowledgments

If I listed all the people who contributed to this book one way or another, it would take pages. In brief, then, let me name four of the most important ones: Sonia Kiser, my sister, who always supports my endeavors in more than one way; Megan Turner, Atmosphere editor, o excellent one; and Jane Blakelock and Lee Huntington, who took time out from busy lives to criticize this latest effort. My heartfelt thanks.

About Atmosphere Press

Founded in 2015, Atmosphere Press was built on the principles of Honesty, Transparency, Professionalism, Kindness, and Making Your Book Awesome. As an ethical and author-friendly hybrid press, we stay true to that founding mission today.

If you're a reader, enter our giveaway for a free book here:

SCAN TO ENTER
BOOK GIVEAWAY

If you're a writer, submit your manuscript for consideration here:

SCAN TO SUBMIT
MANUSCRIPT

And always feel free to visit Atmosphere Press and our authors online at atmospherepress.com. See you there soon!

About the Author

JO ANN KISER, a native of eastern Kentucky, spent several years at *The New Yorker*, where her favorite job was as a fact-checker. Later she returned to school and received a Ph.D. from the University of Chicago's Committee on Social Thought with her dissertation on dialectic and salvation in Marcel Proust's *A la recherche du temps perdu*. Her earlier publications include the novel *A Young Woman from the Provinces* and a collection of short stories titled *The Guitar Player and Other Songs of Exile*.

www.ingramcontent.com/pod-product-compliance
Ingram Content Group UK Ltd.
Pitfield, Milton Keynes, MK11 3LW, UK
UKHW041121090425
457235UK00008B/29/J

9 798891 326316